# RAINMAKER

# RAINMAKER

## ALISON JACKSON

Boyds Mills Press

Published by Boyds Mills Press, Inc.
A Highlights Company
815 Church Street
Honesdale, Pennsylvania 18431
Printed in China


Publisher Cataloging-in-Publication Data

Jackson, Alison.
    Rainmaker / by Alison Jackson.—1st ed.
  [200] p. :   cm.
Summary: After four years of drought, the farmers of Frostfree, Florida are facing
ruin, and raise money to bring a rainmaker to town. Are they placing their hopes
in a dream? Thirteen-year-old Pidge struggles with this and other questions in a
story set in 1939.
ISBN 1-59078-309-3
1. Farm life — Florida — History — 20th century — Fiction — Juvenile literature.
2. Drought Droughts—Economic aspects —Florida — Fiction — Juvenile literature.
[Fic] 22    PZ7.J13217Ra 2005

First edition, 2005
The text is set in 13-point Minion.

Visit our Web site at www.boydsmillspress.com

10 9 8 7 6 5 4 3 2 1

*In loving memory of Samuel Henry Coombs,*
*1916-2001*
*—A. J.*

# RAINMAKER

# I

THAT YEAR THE RAINMAKER came to Frostfree was the year I found out about my mother. It was also the year my little brother got too big for his britches. Before then, I could always count on him to lend me a hand around the house and the farm—or at least keep me company. We'd pick oranges from Papa's fruit trees and eat them right there in the shade, the juice slurping down our chins and forearms. Or sometimes we would walk into town to buy some penny candies or chewing gum.

But everything changed during the summer of 1939. Maybe it was the drought. Months of dry weather can bring out the meanness in a person, even a little person like Little Jack. Whatever it was, he took to sassing me every chance he got. And lately he'd been saying things like "Go jump in a lake" or "Tell me somethin' I don't already know." It was enough to drive a person crazy.

I can actually pinpoint the first day I noticed this transformation. How long it had been brewing was anybody's guess, but that particular Tuesday morning I was in no mood for my brother's nonsense. It was after Independence Day, just about a month before my birthday, and it hadn't rained anywhere in central Florida for nearly four times that long.

Little Jack was pretending to be a soldier, on account of all the fighting he'd heard about going on over in Europe. He would attempt to pelt my legs with tiny green peas, which had fallen on the kitchen floor and gone unnoticed for days, until they were as hard as rock salt. When his aim got better, my temper got worse.

"Get out of here, Little Jack," I scolded. "I need to get this meat loaf in the oven before Aunt Retta wakes up."

"Tell me somethin' I don't already know," he said.

"Well . . . if you don't stop throwing peas at my legs, I'm gonna swat your little bottom."

"Go jump in a lake."

"No dessert for you tonight," I warned.

He thought about that, but not for very long. "See if I care, Pidge."

I abandoned my meat loaf and began walking toward him. "I mean it, Little Jack. I'm fixing to wear you out."

He took off through the screen door before I could even get close to him, and I decided to just let him be. Lately, that boy never listened to a word I said anyway.

My Aunt Retta told me Little Jack was acting this way because he didn't have a mama around, but I thought having me and Retta in the house was like getting two mamas for the price of one. Besides, I didn't have a mama, either, and you didn't see me going around shooting peas at people.

I lost my mother right around the age that Little Jack is now. He was just a baby at the time, but I was seven years old. Old enough to know her, and to miss her. Sometimes I think Little Jack is lucky that way, that he never even had a chance to get acquainted with Mama. But Papa says when Little Jack gets older, he's gonna miss those memories he never had, and at least I've got mine.

Maybe that's why my brother was getting so ornery lately. Maybe he was already starting to want some memories of his own.

One day, when Little Jack was being particularly troublesome about doing his chores, I scolded him and he said, "I don't have to listen to you. You ain't my mama." This took me by surprise, seeing as how he hardly ever mentioned our mother at all.

"You're right," I agreed. "Mama was nothing like me."

That's when Little Jack finally broke down and asked me about her, like he'd probably been wanting to do for some time.

I tried my best to answer his questions, but it was hard to put the things I remembered into words. I knew Mama was tall and thin. And she didn't talk a whole lot. She used to cover her mouth when she laughed, too. I remember that. It was because of her one tooth that had gone a little off-color, after she'd been kicked by a horse as a teenager.

But I thought that tooth was kind of pretty. It made my mother different from everybody else.

Little Jack stopped asking me questions a while ago. It happened around the same time he got a big mouth on him. Maybe he couldn't ask questions and fuss at me all in the same breath. But I wished he would start asking again because his nagging was really getting on my nerves.

My brother slammed the screen door on his way back into the kitchen. He stood beside me, his chin barely clearing the countertop.

"That meat loaf is all lopsided-lookin'," he told me.

"Maybe that's 'cause you're looking at it lopsided."

"Go jump in a lake," he said. Then he added, "You're pitiful in the kitchen anyway. Everybody knows it. You can't cook and you can't sew. You're gonna end up an old maid, just like Aunt Retta!"

I grabbed a bar of soap to throw at him, just as Papa came into the kitchen. He wiped his hands on his overalls a few times and took off his cap. Papa's clothes were damp with perspiration, and his hair was stuck to his head.

"I sure could use a glass of water," he said, which really meant there was still no rain in sight. No one around here liked to talk about the drought directly. It was considered bad luck for citrus growers to comment on the weather. But comment or not, this was the longest drought Frostfree had seen in forty years. Half the farmers in town were living on nothing but hope, and we'd all lose our farms if rain didn't come soon.

"Hey, Papa!" Little Jack shouted. "Pidge is gonna be an old maid!"

"Leave your sister alone," Papa said crossly.

My little brother stuck out his lower lip so far you could yank on it. I don't think he'd yet figured out that Papa's moods were directly related to his orange groves. If the oranges looked bad, Papa got real irritable.

"Your Aunt Retta still napping?" Papa said. He eyed my lopsided meat loaf and made a face. Little Jack nearly died laughing.

"I think so," I said. "You know how her feet swell up in this heat."

"I surely do," Papa said quietly. He poured himself a tall glass of water and drank it down without even stopping.

"*My* feet don't swell up in the heat," Little Jack said. That boy was always fishing for attention.

"That's because your *head's* already swelled up bigger than a watermelon," I replied.

Papa laughed real hard at that one, and my brother scowled.

"Go jump in a lake," he said, running back out onto the porch.

❊   ❊   ❊

Aunt Retta eventually came down for dinner and we sat around the table, not saying much. Little Jack pushed his food around with a fork, but the rest of us didn't even pretend to be eating. Dinner, usually served at noon, was our biggest meal of the day. But it was hard to put food in your mouth when it was so hot and dry outside. The four-month-long drought might as well have been sitting there, right in middle of the table along with the hot rolls and the misshapen meat loaf.

"I'm sorry I couldn't help you make dinner, Pidge," Retta said, wiping her forehead with a napkin. "That swelling got real bad today."

"Your swelling is bad every day!" Little Jack said.

"Mind your manners, Little Jack," Papa warned.

Aunt Retta gave my brother a stern look, a look she had perfected in the seven years she'd been living in our house. My aunt had moved in with us right after Mama died. She was Papa's older sister, although they didn't look a thing alike. And her real name was Marietta Martin, but everyone just shortened it to Retta, so the name sort of stuck. Aunt Retta had never been married or had children, and she loved us just like we were her own. I loved her, too, but not like she was my own mama. I know that sounds mean, but I had a place for my mother and a place for Aunt Retta, and I was happy with that.

"Eat your peas, young man," my aunt said.

"Pidge ain't eating hers," he shot back.

"Am so." I shoved a mouthful of peas into my mouth and chewed real hard.

Papa put his napkin on the table and leaned back. "It's too hot to eat 'em anyway, Little Jack," he said to my brother.

I caught Aunt Retta's eye across the table, my

mouth still full of those wretched peas. I was so mad, I nearly spit them back out on my plate.

Little Jack's face broke into a wide grin. "Pidge can eat all *my* peas, too!" he crowed.

Papa actually laughed a little. "Then she'll grow big and strong," he said. "And you'll be a little squirt forever."

Little Jack was small for his age, and he didn't like being reminded of that. He also looked up to Papa something fierce, wanted to be just like him. My brother quickly jammed a spoonful of peas into his mouth and chased it down with a gulp of milk.

Retta winked at me, then glanced over at Papa. "By the way, Big Jack, I ran into Jenny Barton today, from down at the church."

Jenny Barton played the organ on Sunday mornings and gave piano lessons in town. Papa would chat with her sometimes, after Reverend Tanner's sermons, but I didn't like her much. She'd arrived in Frostfree two years ago with nothing but a suitcase and a piano—and the woman had been trying to talk me into taking lessons ever since. Shoot. It was obvious that she was only chasing Papa—and making a fool of herself in the process.

"Jenny asked how y'all were doing," Aunt Retta prodded.

Papa stretched back in his chair again. "I'm sure she did," he said, and let the subject of Miss Jenny drop.

a while, the name sort of shrunk itself down to Pidge. I never even knew my name was Miriam until I got to the first grade. When the teacher took roll, I wouldn't answer to Miriam, and she finally had to cave in. I've officially been Pidge ever since.

My father's full name is Jack McGill Martin. Not John. Just Jack. And my brother is Jack Jr., but everyone calls him Little Jack. He seems to like it, so we see no reason to change it. By now, Miss Crockett over at the Union Faith Elementary and Secondary School knows better than to argue with any of us Martins about our names anyway. Especially Little Jack. She has bigger fish to fry when it comes to that feisty brother of mine.

Besides, Miss Crockett is lucky that any of us go to school at all. A lot of kids my age don't even bother. By the age of thirteen, they're needed too badly to help on the farms, and they just sort of stop coming to school. Especially this past year.

As if the drought weren't bad enough, Florida had one of its worst frosts this season, too—just last January. Goes to show you that the person who named our little town "Frostfree" was more into wishful thinking than honesty.

The frost nearly killed our entire crop this past year, and school was closed down for a week so we could all stay home and help cover the trees, pack them with dirt, and man the smudge pots. That basically meant staying up all night, filling hundreds of pots with fuel, then firing them up and keeping them burning until the temperatures finally rose above 32 degrees on all of our thermometers. Every single one of those thermometers *had* to read above freezing before we were allowed to sleep because temperatures could vary as much as five degrees, even from one row of trees to the next. Frosts are a local thing, you see, not like freezes, which pretty much cover most of the state whenever a cold front comes through.

To hear Papa tell it, frosts happen when the soil cools down faster than the air. Then the air gives up some of its heat to help the soil out. But the lowest air temperatures still end up closer to the ground, and if the ground freezes, the trees are lost. Now I know this might sound strange, but the higher up a place is, the less likely it is to have a frost.

And, just so you know, Frostfree is about as *low* as you can get. The only hill in this town is barely ten feet above sea level, but we call it *Mount* Frosty. So I guess everybody here is guilty of a little wishful thinking now and then.

We live in Polk County, which is just about smack dab in the middle of the state. Water to the east and west of us. The Florida Keys to the south, and the state of Georgia to the north. Not that I've ever been to any of these places. Nobody around here ever goes anywhere.

On second thought, I take that back. Becky Ramsey, who used to be my best friend, went off to Louisiana last year, and she never came back. Just abandoned the farm and everything. Papa says it was because of the frost, but Aunt Retta told me it was on account of the taxes. When citrus prices fell a few years back, Becky's family just couldn't hang onto their farm anymore.

Sometimes I think they did the smart thing. It's too much trouble, fighting the frosts and then the droughts. In the end, there's nothing we can do to stop either one of them.

But Papa gets angry when I talk that way. For him, our farm is more important than practically anything. About a year and a half ago, he took me for a long walk around the farm, clear out to the end of the orange groves. He stopped, right in the middle of that last row of trees and took my hand.

"All this will belong to you, Pidge," he said, as if he were handing me some sort of present. "As long as you got this farm, you'll never have to take nothin' from nobody."

I didn't quite understand what he meant then, but I guess maybe I'm starting to now. During the past couple of years I've seen families come through this town, looking for work to do on the farms. Most of them don't even ask for money, just a place to stay and some food to eat. Their clothes are patched and worn, washed so many times you can see the stitching through the fabric. And the children work the farms, too, just as hard as the parents. But when it's all done, none of them has anything they can call their own. The only thing they have to look forward to is the next farm, the next job, and the next meal.

So I guess we're not as bad off as some. Leastways, Little Jack and I can walk into town for some new clothes from time to time. And we've never gone a day without food. Maybe I should remind him of that next time he sasses me about my cooking. Or grows too fast for his clothing.

"These shoes are too small," he announced one day. This wasn't news to me. He'd been saying it for three days now, and we were all tired of hearing about it.

Papa handed me two dollars. "Take him into town for some new ones," he said.

I stared down at the two dollars in my hand. How come I wasn't getting new shoes, too, I wanted to know?

But Papa read my mind. "We'll get you some, before school starts," he said quietly, and then I felt guilty. My father had a way of doing that to a person. Maybe it was because he never complained about much of anything at all.

Little Jack and I started out to town along the main road. Pretty soon we were cutting through the woods, though. It was too hot to be anywhere but in the shade. To tell you the truth, I didn't much like walking through the woods. I was scared of snakes. But Little Jack didn't seem to be very worried about them. Before long, I began to relax a little, too. Hey, I figured my brother was making so much noise, he'd probably frightened every snake in Polk County away.

"I'm gonna be a millionaire when I grow up!" he crowed, grabbing a fallen tree branch off the ground and waving it around like a sword. "Just like Daddy Warbucks." My brother and I liked reading *Little Orphan Annie* in the Sunday comics.

"That so?" I said. "And where you gonna get all that money?"

He whacked a tree trunk with his weapon. "Gonna be a movie star."

Little Jack had been to the movies only once. We didn't have but one movie theater in town anyway. And it had been showing the same picture for six months.

"What do you know about being a movie star?" I asked him.

"I know you don't have to stay up all night, minding smudge pots."

He had me there. "Or praying for rain," I added.

He smiled smugly. "Tell me somethin' I don't already know."

We stepped out of the woods into the cemetery behind the Union Faith Community Church. Mama was buried here, and I liked to visit her grave sometimes. But not when I was shackled with Little Jack. My brother was partial to flitting in and out among the gravestones, playing hide-and-seek, and I thought this was disrespectful. But to my relief, he wasn't feeling all that playful today. Maybe this was because he caught sight of two local boys who were playing kick-the-can in the community churchyard. I spied the boys, too, and immediately recognized Denny Harper and his buddy Noah Blore.

Denny was one of those people who always had friends. He'd been that way ever since our first day with Miss Crockett at the Union Faith Elementary and Secondary School. Denny was different now, though. More grown up, but still very popular—especially with the girls.

Noah was admired, too, but in a quieter kind of way. I think he was popular mostly because he was Denny's friend. Denny did most of the talking for both of them. He walked around Frostfree like he owned the place, and everybody just sort of believed it. But Noah spoke to you like you were every bit as important as he was. And he had a way of laughing at things—even Denny sometimes—that I found likeable. Not that I would ever tell *him* that. I had better things to occupy my time than boys.

As Little Jack and I approached them, I saw that a cluster of girls had gathered on the church steps. They were watching the boys as they played.

Oh, no. Right in the middle of the group was Dora Wheaton, the new girl from Atlanta. Well, to be honest, she wasn't really all that new. Dora's family had arrived in Frostfree three years ago, looking to "revolutionize the citrus industry," or so my father liked to say. Dora's father, Dr. Winslow Wheaton, was some sort of farming specialist from Georgia. He'd invented a fruit-washing machine, which most folks around here agreed was pretty ridiculous. Then one day he just upped and decided to leave Atlanta and start up some orange groves—right here in Frostfree—and show all us Florida citrus growers how farming *should* be done.

The man wasn't much liked around here, but his farm was showing a profit, and he was always the first person in town to make charitable donations and help out other farmers in need. Aunt Retta told me that he really wasn't *trying* to act better than the rest of us, but I didn't believe her. Not if his wife and daughter were any examples.

Mrs. Lila Wheaton had been listed in the 1937 edition of *American Women* as an "eminent Georgian artist." She was known for her sculpture and garden pieces, which no one here in Frostfree gave a fig about.

And Dora put on airs that could make your toes freeze. That girl definitely thought she was better than anybody else in Frostfree. All of her clothes were ordered special from a big department store up in Atlanta. And if you ask me, her "Southern belle" act was getting a little stale. You'd think that after three years she could just drop it. But I'll bet Dora practiced batting her eyelashes every night in front of a mirror.

Denny and Noah were the first to notice us.

"Hey, Pidge! Hey, Little Jack!"

Little Jack swung his stick at them. I brushed a quick hand through my hair, to straighten any obvious tangles. Why did my little brother always have to be with me?

Then I waved at them. "What y'all up to?" I said, trying to sound very casual and just the slightest bit bored.

Denny kicked an empty soup container. It clanked against a metal post and bounced off to the left. "What do you think we're up to?"

"No good," I replied.

Noah laughed, but Denny studied me, like he was trying to figure me out.

"Well, it looks to me like *you're* baby-sitting," he said, with his famous grin.

Little Jack scowled up at him. "Go jump in a lake," he said.

Dora and her group of friends giggled from the church steps. They were all sharing orange soda from a bottle. Three straws stuck up from its long neck. One of the girls was Martha Jarvis. She was actually pretty nice, when Dora wasn't around. The other was Jean Hippleton. She used to play dolls and hopscotch with Becky and me, before Dora came to town. The three of us had even made up a secret rhyming game that we played at school. We'd start with a word and then add a word that rhymed, but the phrase had to be a complete sentence. Once Jean and I had gotten all the way up to eight words.

Now she hardly ever spoke to me. Dora had seen to that. Ever since I beat her in the fifth-grade spelling bee, Dora Wheaton seemed determined to get back at me. I'd taken the gold pin, which she felt was rightfully hers. So stealing my best friend was her act of revenge—like for like.

"Oh, he is soooo cute!" Dora cooed at my brother. "Such a little darlin'."

If Little Jack were a dog, he'd have wagged his tail right off. The silly fool didn't even know when he was being laughed at.

"Well, he's not so cute once you get to know him," I said.

I jumped out of the way as Little Jack's stick

made a swat at my leg. This sent Dora and her crew into hysterics. Denny and Noah laughed, too. Suddenly it felt as if *I* were the butt of their joke, and not Little Jack at all.

"Uhhh, I probably ought to get going," I said quickly.

"What's the hurry?" Noah said. "Where y'all goin'?"

"I'm gettin' me some new shoes," Little Jack answered for me. "On account of I'm growing like a *weed*."

Dora examined my brother's worn-out shoes. Just this morning Papa had cut a slit in the sides, so Little Jack wouldn't get blisters walking into town.

"Well, it surely looks like you could use some," she said, in a honey-coated voice.

Dora, Jean, and Martha giggled again, then took dainty little sips from their straws.

My cheeks burned like hot coals. I wanted to kill my little brother right there behind the community church! Let lightning strike me dead.

"Why, what's wrong with your *face*, Pidge?" Dora asked, ever so sweetly. "I think you might be getting a sunburn!"

Jean and Martha tittered innocently, and I grabbed Little Jack's hand.

"Probably the heat," I said quietly, yanking my brother with me as I headed around the church to Fielder Street.

As soon as I was out of sight, I stopped walking and clenched my fists, trying to calm down.

The whole lot of them were probably still laughing about me, I thought. Or worse . . . maybe they'd already dismissed Pidge Martin and her annoying younger brother.

Little Jack scratched a long squiggly line into the sidewalk with his stick.

"Come on, Pidge," he said. "They don't care about us anyway."

For once, I thought my little brother just might be showing some signs of real human intelligence. I knew he was right. But that didn't make me feel any better. Not one lick.

# 3

"How come I gotta wear these trashy old things back home?" Little Jack asked me. We had just entered the leafy overhang of the woods, and I was carrying his brand-new shoes in a plastic bag, slung over one shoulder.

"You don't want to get your new shoes all dirty, now do you?" I asked.

"I don't care," he replied, kicking up a pile of dead leaves and moss.

I suppose I shouldn't have cared, either, but

shoot. I didn't want Papa seeing Little Jack's new shoes all scuffed and dirty the minute we walked through the door.

Little Jack pouted some more.

"These shoes have holes in them," he said. "Dora and them girls were laughing at me."

"No, they weren't," I said.

Little Jack stopped dead in his tracks and gave me a look.

"All right, all right. Maybe they were, just a little. But you gotta consider the source."

"What's that mean?" Little Jack still hadn't budged. He was facing me now, hands on hips and his chin jutting out, just like a riled-up rooster.

"Well . . . it means that you shouldn't even worry about people like Dora Wheaton and what they think about anything. Her opinion isn't worth much."

"But what about Denny and Noah? They was laughing, too."

Were they? I wasn't so sure about that. Denny maybe, but I didn't think Noah would laugh just because a person had a few holes in his shoes. His daddy's farm had nearly gone under a few years back, and he knew what it was like to do without. If it hadn't been for Papa, the Blores would have lost their place altogether. But my father loaned them enough money to see them through picking season, and they'd been mighty grateful ever since.

Fact was, Noah Blore idolized my father and hung onto his every word. That's probably why he was always so nice to Little Jack and me. Leastways, he wouldn't have laughed at my brother's shoes.

I didn't know what to say to soothe Little Jack, though. I felt bad about the laughter, too, even if Dora Wheaton had been the instigator. It hurt when people made fun of you.

"We're poor, ain't we?" Little Jack asked out of the blue. Or perhaps it wasn't so out of the blue. I think his mind had been chewing on this one all the way home.

"No, sir," I said. "We got our own farm. And we got food, and we got clothes. That's a lot more than most people can say, especially in these hard times."

My brother stared down at his shoes and then back up at me. "Dora Wheaton ain't *most* people," he said seriously.

I laughed. "Tell me somethin' I don't already know." And Little Jack laughed, too.

❉    ❉    ❉

When we finally left the woods, the sky was already darkening in the east. Little Jack ran up ahead and then stopped at the entrance to our long, sandy drive. He pointed to a dusty red pickup truck parked in front of our porch.

"Come on, Pidge," he yelled. "We got company!"

By the time I entered the house, Little Jack was already hovering outside the parlor door. I peeked inside, over his head.

"Looks like Mr. Tatum," I whispered. Jeff Tatum owned the farm next to ours. Sometimes he and Papa helped each other out if the citrus groves needed pruning or harvesting. I think Papa even loaned him money from time to time, but I don't know if Mr. Tatum ever paid him back.

At the moment, he and my father were talking quietly, and Mr. Tatum kept pointing at a newspaper that he held in one hand. He seemed excited about something, and Papa was rubbing his palms across his chest—the way he did sometimes when he was being extra thoughtful.

"Your ears are going to fall right off your heads if you stretch them out any farther," Aunt Retta said from behind us. Little Jack jumped nearly a foot into the air.

"You shouldn't sneak up on people like that!" he said.

"And you shouldn't listen in on private conversations, Little Jack Martin. Eavesdroppers never hear anything they *want* to hear. Now, scoot. Supper's almost ready." She turned to me. "I could use some help with the mashed potatoes."

"Yes'm," I said, embarrassed to be caught listening in on Papa.

But Little Jack wasn't embarrassed at all. As soon as we got into the kitchen, he was poking his nose right where it didn't belong again.

"What's Mr. Tatum here for?" he asked, reaching for a piece of corn bread.

"Wash your hands first," Retta scolded. "And that's for your Papa to know. Not you."

"But it ain't picking time yet," Little Jack whined. "And Papa and Mr. Tatum just pruned everything after that big frost."

Aunt Retta's lips were set in a straight firm line. My brother knew he would get nothing out of them, so he went to the sink and washed his hands.

I added some milk and sweet butter to the potatoes and began mashing it all together in a large pot cooling on the stove.

We heard the front door close, and a minute later Papa entered, still rubbing his chest with one hand. In the other he held the newspaper which Mr. Tatum had seemed so fired up about.

"What did Mr. Tatum want, Papa?" Little Jack prodded him.

Papa just stared at my brother without answering him. He walked over to the table, setting the paper down, and a slow smile played at his mouth before he turned his attention back to Little Jack.

"A miracle," Papa said finally, and his smile got even bigger.

"Pardon?"

"Mr. Tatum wants a miracle, son. And I think we're in need of one about now. Don't you?"

Little Jack looked at me, his eyes open wide. I simply shrugged, not sure what to make of my father's strange behavior.

Aunt Retta was all business, as usual. "Well, the good Lord is the only one provides that sort of thing, last thing I heard," she huffed. "Man should get himself on down to church if he wants to see a miracle."

She began setting down plates and silverware, and I helped her. I couldn't keep from sneaking a peak at the newspaper, though, folded up near Papa's end of the table. All I could see was a grainy photograph of an old woman with wire-rimmed glasses, her hair wrapped in a bun. And a few words. Something about *magic* and *into the firmament*. If this was Mr. Tatum's idea of a miracle, I felt sorry for him.

Papa sat down, loading food onto his plate. He hadn't said anything more about the miracle, and I think we were all too afraid to ask. Maybe the heat had finally gone completely to his head. But Little Jack just couldn't stand it any longer.

"What the devil—" he began, but Retta shushed him.

"It's time to say grace," she said. "Big Jack, will you do the honors this evening?"

Papa gazed at my aunt as if he were seeing her through a thick fog. Then he cleared his throat and bowed his head. We did the same.

"Dear Lord," Papa began, "we hope that you will bless us with many things. An end to this economic Depression. Peace over there in Europe. And a miracle for us, right here in Frostfree. A miracle that we so desperately want. Let the skies open up, Lord, and give us the rain we sorely need. Just let it rain. That's all I ask. Be it in your power, or in the power of another, just let it come. Let it come. Let it come. Amen."

Aunt Retta sniffed, then placed her napkin on her lap. "Not much of a blessing, if you ask my opinion," she said.

Which no one had.

Papa picked up the newspaper, turning it in our direction, so that the three of us could see the old lady in the photograph.

"This here is Miss Millie Boze," he said, "and she is a Rainmaker."

I swallowed, not daring to glance over at my aunt. "A Rainmaker?" I repeated.

"Yes," Papa said. He regarded the group of us seated around the table. "I didn't believe it, either, until Jeff Tatum showed me this newspaper article. But it's true. Miss Millie has the power to produce rain."

I could hear Aunt Retta clucking away at her end of the table. Little Jack, for once, was speechless.

"But how—" I began.

"No one knows," Papa said. "She just . . . does it. Look here." He pointed at a paragraph in the article. "She says, 'I just have the power to bring rain, and I can't explain it. I project myself into the firmament and the rain comes.'"

Retta set down her fork. "And you have proof of this, I suppose?"

Papa grinned excitedly. "Yes! I do! Miss Millie has already been summoned by citrus growers in Wauchula and Sebring. It rained in both places within forty-eight hours!"

"But Sebring's not even fifty miles away," I said. "How could it have rained there and not here?"

My father gave his newspaper a vigorous slap. "Miss Millie, that's how!"

"I think this woman must be some sort of con artist," my aunt muttered to Little Jack, but Papa heard her.

"Retta, the woman is sixty-seven years old and practically deaf. Besides, she doesn't charge anything for her services. All she asks for is a place to stay, a meal or two, and a train ticket from Oxford, Mississippi."

I began to feel some of Papa's excitement. Wouldn't it be something if this woman really could bring an end to the drought? And what did we have to lose?

"Is this what Jeff Tatum was here talking to you about?" Aunt Retta asked.

"Yes, ma'am," Papa said, with a firm nod of his head.

"And who is he planning to brainwash next?"

"Joe Hippleton and Will Jarvis," Papa replied, ignoring the "brainwashing" part of her question. Jean's family and Martha's, I thought. "Then Jeb Harper and Nathaniel Blore," he went on. Denny and Noah's parents, too. "And anybody else who's interested. I'm calling a meeting for Thursday evening, down at the church. See how much money we can come up with, among the lot of us."

"Why don't you just let Dr. Wheaton pay for it?" Little Jack suggested, and I thought I detected that familiar ornery note in his voice. My little brother wasn't about to forget Dora's teasing from this afternoon. "Doc Wheaton has more money than *all* y'all put together!"

Papa sighed. "Does indeed," he said quietly.

But I knew Papa wouldn't talk to Dr. Wheaton about Miss Millie. None of the other farmers around here would, either. They were all afraid he'd laugh at them, just the way Dora had laughed at my brother's split-open shoes. Dr. Wheaton's fancy farming methods were based on scientific experiments and predictions, which surely left little room for Rainmakers, even though *most* people in this town weren't above a little bit of superstition now and then.

Well, I thought, recalling my brother's simple statement from this afternoon. The Wheatons were not *most* people now, were they?

# 4

NEWS OF THE RAINMAKER SPREAD across Frostfree quicker than grease on a red-hot skillet. And it was welcome news, too. Gave us something more to talk about than drought, money worries, and the possibility of war.

"Do you really think Miss Millie will come all the way out to a small town like this one?" I asked Aunt Retta on Thursday morning. Thursday was ironing day. As usual, we'd set up the ironing board in the parlor, because it was the only room in our entire house that allowed a breeze. We'd also sent Little Jack over to play with Jimmy Tatum, so he wouldn't be underfoot all the time.

My aunt hated ironing. She snatched one of Papa's denim shirts from on top of the laundry pile and attacked it with the steam iron, like the shirt was alive. Then she let out a little snort.

"Person will do just about anything, if the price is right."

My function in all of this ironing business was to drape the shirts onto clothes hangers after my aunt was finished pressing them. If I found some loose threads or a button missing, I was instructed to stack the shirt onto the sewing pile.

"But . . . isn't rain worth just about any price?" I asked.

Aunt Retta looked up at me and her expression softened a little. "I guess it is, Pidge," she admitted.

I fingered a flower-shaped button on one of Aunt Retta's eyelet blouses. This one was different from all the other buttons on the garment.

"Where'd this button come from, Aunt Retta?" I asked.

"That button was your mama's," she said quietly, and her face melted like butter. "I remember the blouse it came from, too. White cotton, with lace all around the collar."

Papa had probably saved this button, I thought.

He'd saved quite a few of Mama's things—at least those he could still bear having around, once she was gone. My father had given me a box of my mother's belongings about a month after she died. Just carried it into my room and plopped it down on the bed. No explaining. No stories behind the mysterious scarves and keys and jewelry. These things were just mine now, he said. To do with as I saw fit. Papa hadn't given me her wedding ring, though. Mama went to her grave still wearing that.

Aunt Retta stopped ironing. She was gazing out the window, as if she could see something peering in at her through the other side of the glass. "Your mama was just about the sweetest person alive," she said, a smile tickling her lips and eyelids. "Sure did love you and Little Jack, too."

"Is that why she went away?" I asked. "So me and Little Jack wouldn't catch her sickness?"

I could actually see Retta's back straightening. She patted her hair with one hand, the way she did sometimes when she wasn't quite sure what to do or say. My aunt never liked being uncertain about anything.

"Lord no, honey! Your mama's kind of sickness wasn't contagious. Iris just had a little touch of depression, that's all."

Iris. I never thought of her as Iris. The name made me think of a tall fragile flower.

"Like the Depression we're going through now?" I said.

"No, dear. Well, on second thought . . . maybe. You know those men who came through here a few months ago? Asking for work? Remember how tired they looked? Like maybe they should just give up and lie down? Stop fightin' so hard?"

I did. It was in their shoulders, and in the way they walked with heads down, fingers fidgeting at suspenders and hat brims. And in their eyes. Especially their eyes, which didn't see much beyond the task they were finishing or the food they were eating.

"Well . . . what I think is . . . your mama just got tired of fighting. That's all."

"But she came back," I reminded her. "She came home again, so she really didn't give up completely."

Aunt Retta nervously poked a wayward strand of hair behind one ear. "Yes, she surely did, Pidge. I didn't think you'd remembered that."

Well, I hadn't remembered it. Not in a way that I could truly visualize in my mind. I just knew that my mama had tucked me in one night. I'd felt her breath on my cheek and her cool fingers brushing across my forehead. But I'd never told anybody about that evening. Not until now.

My aunt was studying me anxiously, like if she asked me the wrong thing, I might stop talking.

"What . . . what exactly did she say to you, Pidge? Can you remember?"

I reached back into that hazy night, trying to grab at anything. A sentence, a word. But it was so long ago. And I had been half asleep. Shoot, maybe I dreamed the whole thing, but I doubted it.

"No," I said, still playing with the button from Mama's old shirt. "I don't think she said anything at all. It's just a feeling I have, like she was there." Like knowing something you can't prove, I thought.

Retta picked up the iron again, assaulting another collared victim. "Well, I'm glad she got to see you."

Had my mother known she would die that night? Is that why she came home? I was afraid to ask. And, of course, my aunt wouldn't have an answer for me anyway. She hadn't been living with us at the time.

Retta's eyes jumped to the window again, as a dark shadow passed in front of it. I whipped my head around, but whatever—or whoever—it was had already reached the front door.

Papa answered it.

Our visitor was Dr. Wheaton. And behind him stood Dora, all dolled up in a pleated skirt and cotton blouse buttoned clear up to her neck. Didn't that girl know she was standing on an uncovered porch in the middle of the summer?

"Well, Big Jack," Dr. Wheaton boomed gustily, as he strode into the parlor and took a seat on the couch. If he noticed the pile of laundry next to him and the ironing board we'd set up near the fireplace, he didn't let on. "You've certainly given people something to talk about around here."

Papa smiled lazily. Aunt Retta began fussing with her hair again. Dora stood in the entryway, smiling at me. I knew she was itching to get a look at my room upstairs. More for her to laugh about with Jean and Martha. I stayed right where I was.

"How's that, Winslow?" Papa asked slowly.

"Win. You can call me Win, Big Jack. And you must know what I'm talking about. This Rainmaker woman that's got everyone's false hopes all stirred up. Who will you be bringing down here next, Santa Claus?"

He laughed heartily. Papa, leaning one lanky elbow against the fireplace mantel, did not laugh.

"They may have hopes," my father said flatly, "but those hopes ain't necessarily false."

Dr. Wheaton ran a tongue over his dry lips. I willed Aunt Retta not to offer him a glass of water or lemonade.

"This is a fine community, Big Jack," Dora's father said, not unkindly, "with a lot of well-meaning folks in it. You can't ask them to pay their hard-earned money—money that some of them can't even spare—to bring this 'witch doctor' right to their doorsteps. It's like selling a lie, Big Jack. Can't you see that?"

"No, I can't," Papa responded. "All's I see is a whole lot of people with nothing to do but sit around and wait for rain that might never come. At least now they feel like they're doing something. Besides, Miss Millie has been successful—"

"Been lucky is all!" interrupted Dr. Wheaton. "And I won't let you swindle the savings out of every poor farmer in this town."

"I reckon it ain't up to you, Win," Papa replied evenly, but I saw that his hand on the mantel was clenched into a fist.

Aunt Retta smoothed the lap of her dress with her hands. Then she seemed to notice me for the first time. She darted her eyes over to Dora, an obvious attempt to get both of us out of the parlor and away from the adults.

I met her gaze but said nothing, so she gave her head a mighty jerk toward the front door, and I reluctantly led Dora out onto the porch. I was dying to see how this grown-up conversation would end, and I certainly had no desire to make small talk with Miss Dora Wheaton.

Dora had her hair tied back in a braid, and her skin shone pale and smooth. I felt big, clumsy, and dirty next to her.

"Hey," I greeted her uncomfortably, feeling like I was trespassing on my own porch. She just stood there, scrutinizing me and making me feel more than a little self-conscious. I suddenly wished I had worn a cotton blouse today, too, buttoned clear up to my *chin*.

"I like your house," Dora said.

I puffed up with pleasure, until I realized she was just being polite. Shoot. I'll bet Mrs. Wheaton didn't do her family's ironing in the middle of the parlor!

"Oh, it'll do, I guess. Nothin' special, really."

"But that's what's so nice about it," Dora said sweetly. "Everything is so . . . ordinary."

Any self-worth I felt now was quickly evaporating. We stood together on my sun-drenched porch, and I didn't know what to say. I wished I could just run back inside, but I figured that would be too rude.

"Your papa seems kinda angry," I finally offered.

Dora rolled her eyes, as if her father's emotions one way or another held no interest for her at all. Which they probably didn't.

"Oh, sometimes my father can be so . . . proper," she said. Dora's expression flickered then, and I thought I caught a spark of something. Annoyance? Superiority? Was she trying to tell me that my family *wasn't* proper?

At that moment, her father threw the front door open and marched briskly across the wood porch.

"Come, Dora. It's time to leave," he said curtly. Dr. Wheaton glanced at me, then turned and left, Dora following meekly behind him.

And that's when I realized what the girl's eyes had really been trying to convey to me, in that brief moment before Dr. Wheaton had whisked her away. It was embarrassment. She was ashamed, but not for me.

Miss Dora Wheaton had actually been embarrassed for her father.

# 5

THE NEXT MORNING DAWNED SUNNY and cloudless, just like every other morning this summer. The air felt swollen and humid, and my face was covered in a thin sheen of sweat before I was even halfway through my chores. I guess I must have looked pretty worn out, because when Little Jack came downstairs later, he actually helped me clean a few of the kitchen windows without any backtalking.

As we worked, I could see Papa and two other men standing in the orange groves, the backs of their shirts wet with perspiration. Our Hamlins and Parson Browns had been looking small and sickly the past few days, so I was pretty sure that's what all the men were talking about. They were "mapping" the trees, recording how much damage had been done to each, and probably deciding which trees were worth the effort it took to save them.

Most summers there was a layer of reserve water beneath the soil, called the water table. But after so many rainless months, our water table had pretty much run itself dry. In some places, all that empty space under the ground had caused the earth to cave in like a giant crater, taking buildings and sometimes even people with it.

During the last big drought, a sinkhole 35 feet deep had swallowed up half the county prison yard. The sides of the hole were almost vertical, and muddy brown ooze had filled it up overnight. The prison eventually got moved over to Lakeland, and the old site became known as Sinkhole Lake. Now it was a popular swimming spot in Frostfree, especially when school let out. But this summer the lake was shallow and so full of algae that it reeked like rotten cabbage leaves.

My earliest impressions of summer around here always had to do with Papa's oranges—and my trips to Sinkhole Lake. By the time the oranges had begun to "color break," or change from leaf green to yellowish green, I knew school was about to start. And after about a dozen or so swims in the lake, the water would begin to turn dark and cold, as if some muddy creature had churned it up from below and turned the entire swimming hole inside out. That was when I'd begin to feel the first sharp edges of autumn.

Before the drought, I thought these were things that would never change, like the sun coming up every morning. But now I wasn't so sure anymore. I just felt grumpy and out of sorts. I'd been feeling that way all summer.

Suddenly Little Jack said, "The B & B Grocery Store fell into a *giant* sinkhole last night."

I stared at him in amazement. My brother's access to information always took me by surprise.

"Where'd you hear that?" I asked suspiciously.

"Heard Papa talkin' about it." It wasn't often my little brother knew something before I did. He grinned at me, like he'd just swallowed a whole pecan pie and gotten away with it.

"You're lyin'," I said. "Why should I believe you?"

Without warning, Little Jack leaped at me. He beat on my thighs with both hands, until I had to grab his flailing arms in midair.

"What the devil is wrong with you?" I yelled at him.

"*Me*? It's you! You're always acting like you're so

smart," he said. "You think you know everything and that I don't know nothin'!"

How could he say that? After I'd taken him into town for new shoes and listened to all that nonsense about being a millionaire and a movie star. Talk about knowing everything! I should have put him in his place, right then and there.

I took my brother's skinny shoulders in both hands. "What's this all about, Little Jack?" I said.

He wrinkled up his nose and pouted his mouth. "Aunt Retta said you and Papa was talking in private to Dr. Wheaton. About the Rainmaker comin' to town."

So that was it. My brother thought Papa was spoon-feeding me special information that *he* wasn't allowed to hear.

"You're jealous, aren't you?" I said, trying not to laugh.

"Go jump in a lake!"

"Look, Little Jack, I was in the parlor with Papa and Dr. Wheaton, that's all," I said. "Besides, Retta sent me outside with Dora, so I couldn't hear much of anything anyway."

"Why didn't you even *tell* me they was over here?" my brother demanded.

"I don't have to tell you everything!"

"Oh, yeah? Then I guess I don't have to *do* everything you tell me to do, neither!"

Little Jack stormed out of the kitchen and onto the wooden porch. I saw him run across our small expanse of brown lawn, straight toward Papa and the rest of the farmers who were surveying the trees.

My brother said a few words to my father, and they both turned around to face the house. Lord knows what tales that boy was spinning, but when he was finished, Papa put an arm around his birdlike shoulders and Little Jack sped away in the direction of town. My father had probably given him permission to go see the sunken grocery store, and now it would be my job to run and fetch him back.

I leaned heavily against the kitchen counter and glared out the window at Papa's shriveled green-skinned oranges. Shoot! This whole summer was falling into a sinkhole, as far as I was concerned.

*　　*　　*

By the time I got through the woods and into town, quite a crowd had assembled around the B & B Grocery Store. Or what was left of it, anyway. The front half of the B & B was tipped forward precariously, like the forward end of a rocking horse. The sinkhole itself wasn't all that big, but it had definitely swallowed up most of the meat counter and nearly all of the produce.

Mr. Giles, the owner of the B & B, was just standing in the middle of Fielder Street, shaking his head. Mrs. Giles was seated across the road, on the hood of their jet black Oldsmobile. She was crying and pointing at the disaster, while a large group of noisy women crowded around, trying to console her. I couldn't help but notice that the largest and noisiest was Dora's mother, Lila Wheaton.

Miss Jenny Barton, the church organist, was there at the sinkhole, too. She smiled at me, but I pretended not to notice. I knew how sweet she was on Papa, and there was no use encouraging the woman. After all, my father was too busy farming and caring for his family to waste his time on girlfriends.

I spotted Noah and Denny, climbing a wooden sculpture that Mrs. Wheaton had donated to our town two years ago. The monument was actually a carved statue of Robert E. Lee, which she had been working on in Georgia. Personally, I think she couldn't bear having all that work go to waste. So Mrs. Wheaton decided to give it to Mayor Benton, who set it up permanently in an empty lot across the street from the town's biggest and *only* grocery store.

Well. At the moment her artwork wasn't being wasted in the least. That statue now offered the town's best view of the B & B, as it was being swallowed alive.

"Hey, Pidge!" hollered Noah from over one of Robert E. Lee's shoulders. "Come on up!"

I scurried over to General Lee and scrambled up

next to Denny Harper, who was hanging from one of the statue's arms and making loud chimpanzee noises.

"How long y'all been here?" I asked, breathless from the climb.

"About an hour or so," Noah replied.

"Ain't nothin' to see anyway," Denny said, in between his monkey yelps.

I examined the grocery store, which seemed to be falling flat on its face. "Anybody tried to go in there yet?"

Denny stopped swinging. "Can't. The whole thing might collapse."

As if she heard him, Mrs. Giles began a new bout of wailing from across the road. One of the women started fanning her face.

I wondered what Mr. and Mrs. Giles would do now. Their store was nearly gone, and everything in it as well. Come to think of it, what were *we* going to do without a place to shop for groceries?

A horn blast could be heard in the distance, and we all turned our heads to see Dr. Wheaton's silver gray Packard speeding up the road into town. A trail of brownish dust kicked up behind it in a veil, billowing like a parachute when the giant car came to a stop, right in front of the B & B.

Out stepped Dr. Wheaton, his face grim. He took three giant strides across the road, placing a hand on Mr. Giles's arm.

"What's he saying?" I hissed.

Denny and Noah waved their hands impatiently to silence me. But I figured I knew the gist of Dr. Wheaton's words. He was offering the grocer money. Money to help him rebuild his store and to stock the place with food and supplies. Money to get Mr. Giles as an ally.

The way I saw it, Dr. Wheaton probably intended to convince everyone in town that Papa's "Rainmaker" should never set foot in any of our orange groves, and the man needed all the supporters he could get. He was out to prove that Miss Millie Boze was nothing but a liar and a crook. But if that were really true, what did that make my father?

Sure as I live and breathe, Dr. Wheaton returned to his car and grabbed a stack of green bills, right off the front seat. He handed it to Mr. Giles, who took the money wordlessly. Then Mrs. Giles eeked out a sob of gratitude and stumbled toward her husband, who hugged her and proceeded to kiss her—right there in front of God and nearly every citizen of Frostfree, Florida!

"There it goes!" Denny suddenly shouted. Every head turned from the emotional scene in the street just in time to see the B & B Grocery Store crumble like dry sand into a pile of rubble.

A shout went up among the spectators as we watched the earth gobble up Mr. Giles's store. Even

Mr. Giles let out a yell, waving the wad of money he had just received high over his head. I guess he figured he'd gotten the best of that old sinkhole in the end.

People began to disperse once there was nothing left to see but a giant hole in the ground. Eventually Dr. Wheaton's Packard took off down the road, and Mr. and Mrs. Giles piled into their black Oldsmobile. But the three of us stayed right where we were— until the departing cars appeared no bigger than two specks of dust on the road out of town.

Denny made a few more chimpanzee noises, and then I heard a voice from down below us.

"Yoo-hoo! What y'all doin' up there?"

I peeked under General Robert E. Lee's armpit to see Dora Wheaton standing beneath us. Holding her hand and looking very agitated was my little brother.

"I found somethin' that I do believe belongs to you, Pidge," Dora said sweetly.

"I don't belong to *her*!" Little Jack grumbled, trying to rip his hand from Dora's grasp. "She's ugly! She can't even cook . . . and she's gonna end up bein' an old maid!"

Denny laughed so hard, he nearly fell off the statue. Noah smiled silently. I wanted to kick Little Jack from here to kingdom come.

"Why, Little Jack," Dora clucked. "Don't talk that way about your sister!"

He *always* talked that way about his sister, but I guess Dora didn't know that, seeing as how she still wasn't giving up.

"Now you go on and apologize to Pidge right now, y'hear me?" she said to my brother.

Little Jack scowled and began squirming something fierce. Dora held onto him for dear life, and by this time even Noah had begun to laugh.

Little Jack finally broke free and ran around the statue, until he was staring up at me—and General Lee's behind.

"I'm sorry you're such a big ugly cow!" he shouted.

With that, Little Jack tore off down the street and around the corner toward the woods.

Dora giggled helplessly. "Well . . . he did say he was sorry . . ."

The three of us climbed down. I was painfully aware of my stained overalls, as I stood next to Dora in her plaid jumper, which was completely free of dirt or wrinkles.

"Aren't you going to chase after him?" she asked. I studied her face to see if she was laughing about the "big cow" remark, but I didn't think so.

"Nah. He'll get himself home all right."

Noah put his face up close to mine and grinned. "Is it true you can't cook?"

"Course she can cook," Denny said. "She ain't got no mama to do the cookin' for her!"

The grin disappeared from Noah's face, and Dora sucked in a tiny breath of air. I think even Denny knew he'd gone too far this time.

"I can cook tolerable enough when I need to," I said, turning to follow my brother's route into the woods. My face felt hot. I sincerely wished I had just gone ahead and chased after Little Jack the moment he'd taken off.

But Dora scurried after me, plucking at the suspenders of my overalls. I whipped around, good and ready to punch her in the stomach if she said one word about my mama.

"Denny doesn't use his head sometimes," she said quietly. "Everybody knows it."

I kicked a rock with the toe of my shoe, avoiding her gaze. "Everybody except *him*," I said.

And Dora laughed. I felt grumpy and mean, facing her. Maybe Little Jack was right, I thought. Maybe I *was* ugly.

"Hey," I said grudgingly, "that was a fine thing your daddy did back there—helping Mr. Giles and all."

Now it was Dora's turn to blush. "Oh . . . I don't know," she said. "I reckon your daddy would've done it, too, if he could."

She swiveled quickly and trotted on back to Denny and Noah, who were both looking a little ashamed of themselves after Denny's thoughtless comment. I'll bet all three of them were just waiting to see if I'd break down and cry. Well, shoot! If I did, it sure wouldn't be for an audience.

"See y'all around," I said, and Denny seemed relieved that I was still speaking to him at all. Noah gave me a wave and looked as if he were about to say something. But I cut him off with a nod, both hands buried deep inside the pockets of my overalls. I started toward home, trying to put Dora and the boys out of my mind for a while.

But as I entered the woods, I couldn't help thinking about what Dora Wheaton had said. Maybe she really believed that her father wasn't acting better than all the rest of us. But how could she *not* know how it made us feel, seeing him flaunt his money around town like that? Or maybe I was the one who had it all wrong. Perhaps Dora's father had offered Mr. Giles that money out of pure charity, and nothing else.

But I could still see Dr. Wheaton's face that day in our parlor, as he told Papa he was selling a lie to the people in this town. Now, who was really lying, I asked myself? And I also couldn't help but wonder . . . who was doing the selling?

# 6

$B$Y THE TIME I GOT HOME, I was feeling hot, tired, and resentful. Sure, Dora had tried to be friendly back there in town. But she was probably just pretending to feel sorry for me because my daddy was poor and my mama was dead. That girl had no idea what it was like to be me. To her, I was nothing more than Little Jack's baby-sitter. Why else had she dragged him on over to me like that? Humiliating the both of us by saying she had something that *belonged* to me?

Of course, the scene with Dora at General Lee's statue had no lasting effect on Little Jack at all. As soon as I opened the front door, I could hear him carrying on to Aunt Retta, occupying the center of attention as usual.

"That Miss Dora Wheaton?" he was saying. "She showed me all over town. Got me an ice cream down on Delaney Avenue and everything. Then she took me to see the B & B, right before it fell into the sinkhole."

I entered the kitchen and poured myself a tall glass of water, drinking it down in three gulps.

"Go easy with that," Aunt Retta warned me. "The well water's down nearly two feet."

I set the empty glass on the table with a thud. What did she want me to do? Pour it back into the tap?

"Little Jack tells me the B & B sank clean into the ground," Retta continued, giving me a rigid scowl. "Did you happen to see Hank or Nancy Giles while you were there?"

"Yes'm, I did," I answered. "Mrs. Giles was taking it pretty hard."

My aunt groaned softly. "Lord knows, times are hard enough without something like that happening to a person."

Little Jack stepped out in front of me. "Well, Mrs. Giles cheered up some, after Dr. Wheaton gave them all that money."

Retta aimed a look at me over Little Jack's head. "What money?"

My brother couldn't stop himself now. "Oooooh, Dr. Wheaton came driving right down the middle of Fielder Street in his fancy silver-colored car. And the front seat was all filled up with money—"

"I think he just loaned Mr. Giles some money to help him rebuild the store," I finished for Little Jack, surprised that I had said anything like this at all.

Why was I trying to make Dr. Wheaton come out sounding any better than he really was? That man was spreading charity around Frostfree thicker than peanut butter on toast, and here I was lying about it to my own aunt. Was it because of Dora? Well, shoot. I didn't owe her any favors, even if she had been nice to me this afternoon. Was it Papa, then? Maybe I was afraid Aunt Retta would charge right out there to the orange groves this very minute and tell my father all about Doc Wheaton and the money he was willing to spend on grocery stores—instead of on "Rainmakers."

But Aunt Retta saw right through my little white lie. I could never get anything past that woman. "Well, *if* it really was a loan, I'm sure Dr. Wheaton had his reasons for lending Hank Giles a hand," she said, letting me know that certain grown-up matters were none of my business. "After all, charity starts at home, or so they say."

"I didn't hear nobody say that," Little Jack piped up.

"That's 'cause you were too busy talking," I informed him.

My brother said, "Go jump in a lake!" and ran out across the porch and lawn, disappearing into the orange groves. He was probably looking for my father.

I turned to Aunt Retta. "You gonna tell Papa about Dr. Wheaton and that money?"

"Reckon he'll know about it by sundown," my aunt said, and she was right.

*     *     *

Just before supper, Mr. Tatum's red truck pulled into our drive and rolled to a stop in front of the wood porch. Following right behind was Mr. Hippleton's blue pickup, and behind *that* was Mr. Jarvis's rickety old Chevy. From the kitchen window, all I could see was a ribbon of headlights, weaving its way down the road toward our farm, like cat's eyes in the dusk.

Throwing down my spoon, I abandoned the biscuits I'd been mixing and ran out onto the porch, my hands still covered in flour. Aunt Retta was not more than two steps behind.

Papa was standing by Mr. Tatum's truck, talking

to a group of men, most of whom I recognized. Noah's daddy was there, along with Denny's. And more men were walking up the drive from their cars and trucks, all of them grim-faced and silent. Papa's face was drained and tired, as it had been for most of the summer. The other men were talking excitedly to him, but from where I stood on the porch, I could only make out the up-and-down cadence of their voices.

"What do you think they want?" I asked my aunt.

Her hand wavered nervously near her hair. "I couldn't say, honey."

"They look pretty angry."

"Oh, no. I'm sure it's only . . ." Her voice dropped off and I didn't ask again. I was fairly certain this had something to do with the collapse of the B & B, and about Dr. Wheaton and where his money was and was not going—*and* the Rainmaker *and* the drought *and* the failing crops and just about everything else that had been plaguing our town for the past four months or so. Everyone was just fed up.

I was tempted to go back inside, but Retta gently clasped my arm. "Forget the biscuits for now, Pidge. Let's enjoy the evening," she said, leading me to the two wicker rockers under the big parlor window. We sat and rocked, watching the glow of some of the men's cigarettes as the sky grew dark.

"Hey down there!" called a voice from over our heads.

I tilted my head back. Little Jack was hanging from a branch of the oak tree, which draped lazily over one side of the porch.

"Get out of that tree!" Aunt Retta snapped. "You could break your neck, swinging around like that."

"Tell me somethin' I don't already know," Little Jack retorted, but he made no move to abandon his spot on the branch. He was watching Papa and the men, too.

One by one, the visitors began to get back into their cars and trucks. Each of the cars used the driveway to turn around, then the caravan drove away as silently as it had come, its ribbon of tail-lights glowing like distant red embers—until they were swallowed from view by the darkness and the woods beyond.

Jeff Tatum was the last to leave. He took a final puff on his cigarette, then threw it to the ground and stamped on it. He shook hands with Papa—a long unhurried motion—with a pat on Papa's arm thrown in. Then he eased his lanky body into the truck and backed out of the drive, too.

Papa watched quietly as the truck drove off, the big black tires spewing gravel and sand in their wake. Finally, he stepped up onto the porch and made his way over to us.

"What do they want, Papa?" I asked.

Papa sighed and shook his head. "They still want their miracle, darlin'."

I heard Aunt Retta let out a snort beside me. "What's that got to do with you?" she said.

My father leaned against the porch rail. I couldn't see his face, but I could tell that he was smiling. "Well . . . seems like I'm the only one around here with much collateral."

"What's collat—" I began.

"It's property that's worth more than a spit and a promise," Retta said angrily. "Now, Big Jack, don't tell me you're fixin' to take a loan out on your farm, just so these men can pay for a Rain Lady!"

Papa laughed. "Not a loan, exactly. They just wanted to know if I'd be willing to help a few of them out, if we do decide to send for her. They'll pay me back later—when the rains come."

"When the *rains* come? And when will that be? Lord help us all!" My aunt entered the house and slammed the door behind her. Papa and I stared after her in the dim light of the porch lamp. Neither of us said anything.

Suddenly, we heard a loud thump as Little Jack swung himself down from the oak branch and landed heavily on the wooden slats of the porch.

"Why, Little Jack," Papa said, feigning surprise. "Where'd you come from?"

"I climbed up into that tree, all by myself. I was *way* up there, wasn't I, Pidge?"

"Yes, sir," I answered, tired of his antics.

"I'll bet you couldn't do that, Pidge."

I contemplated my brother's tiny outline, standing there on the darkened porch. Shoot, I thought. Any old *fool* could climb that scrawny oak tree. And I had half a mind to tell him so, too. Right this very minute. I mean, here he was, this skinny little runt that I'd been so angry at this afternoon for humiliating me in front of Denny Harper and Noah Blore. And now? Well . . . I guess somewhere between then and now I had just stopped being mad at him. Maybe it was seeing all those men, so desperate for rain they were willing to gamble everything they had for it. So I guess we're all fools, in one way or another.

"No. I sure couldn't do that, Little Jack," I said. "You know, you're probably the best tree climber in all of Polk County."

Even with no moon in the sky, I could see my brother's tiny frame getting taller and taller.

"Tell me somethin' I don't already know," he said.

※　※　※

As difficult as it was for any of us to admit, the drought was actually getting worse. And the orange groves weren't the only casualty now. Folks couldn't get fresh produce at all anymore. For supper, Aunt Retta took to preparing canned greens, the vegetables we were normally forced to eat during the last dry months before spring.

One day I went to the bin out back to get some snap beans for supper, and there weren't any. Not a one. All I could see, after rooting around, were a few cans and jars with year-old grime stuck to the labels. Nothing left but ancient carrots, peas, and green beans.

I suddenly started to cry, right there on the back porch. What would we do when the entire larder was empty, I thought? Would we lose the farm? Would we starve to death? I'd seen those families standing in the free-food line on Saturdays. I'd seen men out of work and kids forced to leave school, just to have something to eat. Would that be us in a few months? Would Papa have to abandon this farm and move us out to Tampa? Or Atlanta? Or Shreveport? I thought about Becky's family in Louisiana and wondered what they were doing now.

After I'd been gone awhile, Aunt Retta came out back, searching for me. She found me, still in tears, sitting at the bottom of the porch steps.

"Pidge, honey? Where are the beans I sent you to fetch?"

"There aren't any," I said, and I burst into tears all over again.

"Oh, my." Aunt Retta wrapped both her arms

around me and let me cry myself dry. When I was finished, she went to the bin and drew out a jar of carrots instead. Then we both walked inside to join Papa and Little Jack for supper. Little Jack got an eyeful of me and slammed down his fork.

"What's wrong with Pidge?" he shouted, before Papa had a chance to shush him.

"It's nothing serious," my aunt assured him. "We're plum out of snap beans, that's all." But I didn't miss the meaningful glance she shot at my father, thinking I hadn't noticed. It was a look that said if we were out of those already, what would we be out of next week? Or next month?

Without a word, Papa stood and walked over to the telephone on the kitchen wall. After dialing a number, he waited a moment before speaking.

"Hello, Jeff? It's Jack Martin. Sorry to trouble you during supper and all, but I thought you should know. I'm sending for Miss Millie Boze, first thing in the morning."

Papa sat back down at the table and smiled broadly at the three of us. No one smiled back.

Then he shook out his napkin and carefully spread it on his lap. "Now, Retta," he said brightly, "how's about some of those delectable carrots of yours?"

# 7

By the next morning, all of Frostfree knew that the Rainmaker was coming to town. Papa had collected money from those who could spare it and borrowed the rest, using our farm as *collateral*. Aunt Retta's earlier definition of that word had left me a bit perplexed, but now I had it pretty much figured out. Basically, the farm was my father's collateral, and he would be forced to give it up if he couldn't repay the loan. But he couldn't repay the loan if we had no crops to sell. And we sure wouldn't have any crops to sell, if it didn't rain soon.

By noon, Papa had wired a telegram to Miss Millie, requesting that she pay us a visit. And by 2:00, Little Jack was driving us all crazy.

"When's she coming?" he kept asking. "Can I meet her at the train station? Could she stay here at our place? Miss Millie can have my room if she wants, but Pidge's room has a better view of the orange groves—"

"Ain't nobody taking over *my* room!" I exclaimed. Where had my brother ever gotten the notion he could just up and give my bedroom away?

Aunt Retta finally suggested that I take Little Jack on over to Sinkhole Lake to get himself worn out.

"But there's no water in that lake," I complained. "It's nothing but a mud pit."

"Fine, then," she snapped. "You can entertain your brother here."

I took him to the lake.

We walked slowly through the woods, pitching rocks at the squirrels as they scrambled up tree trunks.

Little Jack picked up a pine cone and aimed it at one. "Look at me, Pidge! I'm gonna be a baseball player when I grow up!"

His pine cone not only missed the squirrel, it also missed the entire tree.

"Not a pitcher, I hope," I said gloomily.

"Nope. Catcher, I reckon. That way, I can be

right there to see all the hittin', and I can make secret hand signals with the pitcher, too."

Why not, I thought? He had a better chance at baseball than at being a movie star.

The route to Sinkhole Lake was free of leaves or branches, and the two of us made our way easily. As we drew nearer, we could hear laughter—and the sound of splashing water. Who would be crazy enough to swim in that festering swamp during a summer like this one, I thought?

But when my brother and I turned a corner into the clearing, we saw that the banks of the lake were already crowded with people. What was going on?

Little Jack spotted his new friend, Dora Wheaton, in the throng, and he immediately raced over to her.

"Well, hey, Little Jack!" she cried, laying an outstretched hand on top of his blond head.

I don't know why, but it gave me the creeps watching her touch my brother. I still didn't trust Dora completely, and I wondered what she wanted with a seven-year-old kid anyway. Was she planning to steal *him* away from me, too, the same way she'd helped herself to my best friend?

Dora caught sight of me and waved. I waved back cautiously. Then I felt someone grab me from behind. I let out a scream and instantly heard loud laughter back there.

"Hey, Pidge!" Denny said, giving my suspenders a good hard thwap against my back. "Did you come to see Big Al?"

I turned to stare at him, as if he were half crazy. "Big who?"

"Big Al. He's an eight-foot-long alligator that made his way over to Sinkhole Lake!"

Almost *any* body of water in Florida had alligators in it somewhere, but I'd never heard of this fellow, "Big Al." I wondered if Denny might just be making him up to scare me.

"How do you know there's an alligator in this lake?" I asked him doubtfully.

"Mr. Hippleton saw him just this morning, when he was fishin'," Denny answered, a note of pride in his voice. "Came running home in a big hurry!"

Well. That explained the crowd of people on the shoreline. Everyone was waiting to catch a glimpse of the eight-foot-long alligator. I had no intention of going anywhere near it, however. And I hoped Little Jack didn't, either.

I quickly scanned the lakeside for my brother, and when I couldn't catch sight of his white-blond thatch of hair, I rushed into the crowd headlong.

"Little Jack!" I screamed. "Where are you?"

"I'm right here, you scaredy-cat!" he called back, and I saw him over on the other shore, holding tight to Dora's hand. She wiggled a few of the fingers from her free hand at me.

"Come on over here, Pidge," my brother yelled. "You aren't scared of a little old gator, are you?"

The chortling and coughing from behind told me all I needed to know. Denny and Noah were still following close on my tail, and as usual Little Jack had made me out to be the fool, right in front of them. Maybe I should just tell Dora to shove him on into the lake with Big Al.

Over on the other shore, Dora and my brother had taken a seat atop a big rock, both of their heads turned downward in search of the gator. Shoot! No alligator was going to pop his head up out of the water with twenty or thirty people standing there. Gators are actually pretty timid creatures, until you get them riled up. Of course, no one was better at *riling* than my little brother.

Noah, Denny, and I made our way to the rock and climbed up one side. That's when I noticed Martha Jarvis and Jean Hippleton, sitting close to Dora and a little behind her. Neither one of them had said more than two words to me all summer, but I nodded at them anyway. I knew that Jean's father was one of the men in town who couldn't offer any money for the Rainmaker. And she probably felt bad about her family having to borrow from Papa.

"Hey, Pidge," Jean said quietly.

"Hey, Jean," I replied. "Heard your daddy was the one found Big Al down here in the lake this morning."

Jean giggled nervously. "Nearly scared him out of his pants," she said. "He dropped his fishing pole in the water and ran all the way home."

I laughed. Dora Wheaton did, too, and I realized that she was listening in on our conversation. So was Little Jack.

"Awww, I ain't scared of no gator!" he said defiantly. This got quite a laugh from the crowd, especially from Denny.

"Well, sir," Denny shouted. "Guess you wouldn't mind taking a little swim with him then!"

Before I could even let out a squawk, Denny had yanked my little brother up by both armpits and started to swing his flailing stick legs out over the muddy waters of Sinkhole Lake.

Little Jack set to kicking and screaming, but he couldn't get himself free. Meanwhile, Denny was grinning like a cat, and most everyone else was laughing—as if terrorizing a seven-year-old was the funniest thing they'd seen since Charlie Chaplin.

"You let him be!" I shouted at Denny. "Find somebody else to pick on!"

Denny set my brother down as quickly as he had scooped him up. "You mean like *her*?" he shouted, grabbing Dora and swinging her body over his back like a sack of hay.

Dora began beating on his shoulder blades with tiny balled-up fists. "Stop it, you big bully!" she said, but I could hear the laughter in her voice, and I knew she was enjoying every minute of this spectacle. Probably because she was smack dab in the middle of it.

Little Jack had scrambled over to me the minute Denny set him free, and I felt his fingers wrapping themselves around mine. His face was wet with tears, not from fear—but from shame. One thing I had to admit about Little Jack. He wasn't afraid of much. In fact, he was fearless to the point of foolishness. But he knew when people were laughing at him, and he didn't like it one bit.

Neither did I, come to think of it. But I began to wonder if being ignored might actually be worse. I watched Dora giggling and pounding on Denny's back, her pointed toes kicking up and down daintily, and all I could think was: Why hadn't he picked *me* up instead?

But I knew why. I had tried to rescue my little brother from Denny, instead of simply laughing at the joke along with everybody else. And for some reason, this made me angry at Little Jack.

"Why do you always have to go and ruin my life?" I said to him, releasing his tiny hand as if it were crawling with worms.

My brother squinted up at me, like I'd slapped

him across the face. Then something dawned on him, and his eyes narrowed even further.

"If you don't want me ruining your life, then why'd you try and save me?"

That did it. I burst into tears, right there at Sinkhole Lake. What was wrong with me this summer anyway, I wondered? One minute I'd be mad as a hornet and the next thing you knew, I was more protective than a mama lioness with her cubs. I wanted people to pay attention to me, then I got all tongue-tied when they *did*. And lately I'd been crying when I least expected it, for no good reason. But right here in public? With half the kids from my school standing around? This had to be my most humiliating moment yet.

Nobody noticed any of it, of course. They were all too busy laughing at Dora and Denny, shouting at him to throw her into the water. Shoot. I might as well have been invisible. And I might as well go on home, too, before somebody tried to toss Little Jack in there again.

"Are you all right?" Noah said from beside me. Now, when had he gotten himself over here? And why *now*, of all times? When I was blubbering like a baby?

"I'm fine," I assured him. "Just a little shook up is all."

Noah studied me for a long moment, but he

didn't say anything. Instead, he knelt down next to my brother. How about you, Little Jack? Did Denny scare you when he held you out over the water like that?"

Little Jack looked insulted. "I ain't scared of no gator!" he repeated, as if saying this enough times might convince not only Noah, but himself.

Noah laughed. "Don't I know it!" he said. Then Noah stood up again, holding his hand out for my little brother to shake. "Well, you take care of yourself, y'hear, Little Jack?"

My brother nodded seriously and Noah began to walk away before taking one last glance back at us. "You, too, Pidge," he said.

But before I could respond, he was off to join Denny and the rest of his friends gathered around Sinkhole Lake.

# 8

MISS MILLIE BOZE ARRIVED on a Saturday morning in late July. The entire family, dressed in our Sunday best, piled into Papa's pickup to meet her at the station. My usual braids had been let down into long ringlets, and I'd even swiped a bit of lipstick across my mouth when Aunt Retta wasn't anywhere nearby.

Unfortunately, we ran into problems long before reaching the center of town. For one thing, there wasn't anyplace for Miss Millie to sit on the return trip, what with my father and Retta taking up the front seat and Little Jack and me squeezed into the back, like corn in a press.

"Little Jack, you're going to have to sit in Pidge's lap on the way to Miss Millie's hotel," Papa said over his shoulder.

"There's not enough room for my *own* lap in my lap," I groused.

"That's 'cause you're hoggin' the whole backseat!" said Little Jack.

"Well . . . you can sit in Retta's lap then," Papa suggested to him.

My brother's lips puckered into a frown that was the spitting image of Retta's mouth at times. I'd never noticed the resemblance before. He didn't say anything, but I knew what he was thinking. Boys his age were too big to be sitting in anyone's lap—most especially their aunt's.

"Never mind," I said. "I can walk home. It's okay."

Little Jack flashed me a grateful smile, just as Papa slammed his foot down on the brake pedal. Aunt Retta let out a little squeal, and we skidded to a halt.

"What in tarnation!" Papa exclaimed.

We didn't know it then, but our family was caught in the middle of Frostfree's first traffic jam. Cars were stopped in front of us *and* in back of us, all lined up like dominoes on the road into town. And every single vehicle was headed for the train station—to meet the Rainmaker.

Papa leaned his head out the window, then drew it back in like a turtle. "I guess we'll just have to wait our turn, like everybody else," he grumbled, but I could hear the smile in his voice. Big Jack Martin had really started something in this town.

The truck inched forward, and we could see Mayor Benton directing traffic up ahead, sweat dripping down his face—like his head had sprung a leak.

"I can *walk* faster'n this!" Little Jack announced, starting to open the back door of the pickup.

"You're not going anywhere, young man—" Aunt Retta began.

"Aww, let him go," Papa said. "He's just excited is all."

Well, who *wasn't* excited? Miss Millie's arrival was the biggest thing that had happened in Frostfree since President Coolidge passed through in 1929. And I wasn't about to miss her grand entrance on account of traffic!

"Can I go on ahead, too?" I asked.

Retta's eyes gave me the once-over, like I'd lost every ounce of sense I ever had. "Your pretty new dress will get all dusty," she sniffed. But I noticed my aunt had not said no.

Little Jack and I tumbled out of the back and took off in the direction of the train station. We ran past the statue of General Lee and the roped-off sinkhole, where Mr. Giles's B & B Grocery Store once stood. Up ahead, we could see flags and banners strung across Fielder Street. And on the platform, the Ladies' Auxiliary had constructed an arbor of palmetto fronds for Miss Millie to walk under as she exited the train.

A sign had been erected in front of the station, too. It read: *Welcome Miss Millie Boze, the Rainmaker!* Standing right under it, like a welcoming committee, sat Denny Harper and Noah Blore. Noah was dressed up real nice in a jacket and a tie. I tried not to stare at him, but I couldn't help myself. He looked so handsome and grown-up.

"What took you so long?" Denny shouted. "We've been here for hours!"

Little Jack and I ran up to them both, out of breath. "There's a line of cars a mile long back there," my brother said, and for once he wasn't exaggerating.

Noah was gaping at me, and I felt the heat rise in my cheeks. That was when I remembered I was wearing a dress. And lipstick.

"What happened to *you*?" Denny said.

Oh, boy. Where were the sinkholes when you needed them, I thought? At this very moment I gladly would have been swallowed up by one.

Noah just blinked and said, "Your hair looks real nice, Pidge."

I, of course, said nothing. I couldn't. It was like my tongue had just slithered down my throat and lodged itself there.

Denny exploded into a gutteral laugh. "Pidge'll be giving Dora a run for her money soon if we don't watch out!" Was Denny paying me a compliment? Or was this just another of his jokes?

I didn't have time to find out because Little Jack pointed a finger behind me and shouted, "Here comes Dora now!"

I cast a quick glance at Noah. Our eyes connected briefly. Then he suddenly took to examining the tips of his fancy dress shoes.

Dora approached us leisurely, as if she had nothing better to do than pick her way through this crowd gathered at a train platform. What was that girl up to anyway? She seemed totally unaware of the noise, the people, the buzz of excited voices.

"Has Miss Millie arrived yet?" she asked, trying not to sound too interested. And I suddenly knew why Dora was acting this way. Her father must be here in the crowd somewhere.

Doctor Wheaton had pointedly refused to have anything to do with the planning of these festivities. He did not believe in "Rainmakers" or in Miss Millie, and had probably instructed Dora to feel the same way. But did she? How could Dora not be swept up—even a little—by the hum of the crowd? How could she not want to be a part of it all?

But, of course, she did. Why else was she here?

In the distance we could barely make out the faint sound of a train whistle, and the crowd let out a roar. People behind us began shoving their bodies toward the train platform, and it was all we could do to keep our balance.

"Make room! Make room!" I heard a voice shouting. Make room for what, I thought? And then I saw my father and Mayor Benton pushing themselves between the onlookers, trying to get through to the platform. Papa held a pale pink corsage for Miss Millie, while the mayor carried a giant key to the city, carved out of wood by Mr. Fenway, a local carpenter in the town's chamber of commerce.

We saw the black plume of smoke before we caught sight of the engine itself. People began waving anything they could find over their heads: hats, handkerchiefs, even newspapers. I wished I had something to wave, too.

Papa and Mayor Benton finally stepped onto the platform. They stood under the arbor, their backs framed by palmetto leaves.

"Isn't this exciting?" I said to Dora. She didn't reply, but I could see that her eyes were bright and her forehead was slick with sweat.

Denny, who was in front of us, scooted aside to let Dora move in closer. "Can you see all right?" he asked her.

Shoot. There wasn't anything to see yet. And why hadn't Denny made room for me, too?

Noah took a few steps back to stand next to me and my brother. He had that little half-smile on his face, the one that said Denny was impossible to figure out, so why bother? I smiled back. Then Noah reached down to hoist Little Jack onto his shoulders. My brother hooted and hollered, waving his fists in the air like tiny trees in the wind.

The approaching train grew louder, and so did the crowd. Mayor Benton turned to face us, making futile gestures for us to quiet down. Then the train let out a blast louder than thunder, drowning out all conversation as the heavy wheels began to slow, the brakes defiantly squealing their way to a stop.

A cloud of smoke from the engine enveloped the platform, covering Papa and Mayor Benton like an airy cloak. When it cleared, a door in the second car opened and a frail woman with wire-rimmed glasses and a white straw hat stepped hesitantly onto the descending step. Papa immediately reached up to take her elbow, and she smiled gratefully up at him.

This was our miracle, I thought? Why, she didn't weigh more than eighty pounds soaking wet. And she certainly didn't look magical. But at least she didn't look much like a "witch doctor," either. I had known Papa's Rainmaker would be old, of course, but I wasn't sure that the rest of the town had been given any hints as to her age or appearance.

The crowd below was actually silent. They were waiting for our new visitor to speak, I supposed. but the woman seemed to be struck dumb at the sight of all these people gathered here in anticipation of her arrival. I was suddenly very afraid that Miss Millie might keel over right in front of us, before she could even bring the rain we'd brought her *here* for.

"Are you Miss Millie Boze?" asked Mayor Benton, evidently as surprised as the rest of us by her fragile form.

Miss Millie Merely smiled at him, clearly not understanding his question at all.

"Well, shoot," Denny muttered under his breath. "The old bat is senile."

"Shush!" Dora giggled, giving him a little punch in the arm.

Papa whispered something in the mayor's ear, and the two men stepped directly in front of Miss Millie's line of vision.

"ARE YOU MISS MILLIE?" the mayor repeated, only louder this time.

Miss Millie immediately nodded in comprehension, taking the giant key from Mayor Benton and handing him her suitcase. "Yes, I am. Thank you, young man. Could you please take me to the residence of Mr. Big Jack?"

At this, the crowd erupted into a roar of laughter.

"She thinks Mayor Benton is some kind of hired hand," Noah whispered to me, and I laughed, too.

Then, in a grand gesture, Papa held out his hand to the Rainmaker. "Mr. Big Jack Martin, at your service, ma'am," he said, grinning broadly. When confronted by her expression of complete confusion, he repeated himself a little louder, and the woman proceeded to shake his hand.

"Why, she's deafer than a brick wall!" Little Jack said incredulously.

"You don't have to hear to make it rain," I answered defensively. I didn't want my brother thinking any less of Papa, just because he had invited a deaf woman here to perform a miracle. But I should have known better than to assume Little Jack would ever think ill of Papa.

"Well," he said, after a long pause, "I'll bet she can *see* really good, though."

Noah's shoulders lurched in a sudden laugh, nearly letting my brother fall. I grabbed Little Jack from behind, setting him straight again. But I managed to keep my laughter to myself.

The mayor drew a sheet of paper from his pocket. I groaned inwardly, seeing at once that he had prepared a speech for Miss Millie, a speech she would not even be able to hear.

Mercifully, Mayor Benton folded the paper and returned it to his pocket. Even he could tell when it was time to keep his mouth shut.

Instead, Papa presented Miss Millie with her pink corsage. She beamed at him, obviously smitten, and I couldn't help thinking what a fine figure my father made up there, in his Sunday suit and shoes.

"CAN I GET YOU ANYTHING?" Papa said to Miss Millie, when he had finished pinning the flower to the collar of her dress.

She thought for a moment, then said sweetly, "Perhaps a glass of orange juice?"

At this, the entire town of Frostfree let out a giant cheer. If Dr. Wheaton were anywhere about, I sure hoped he was cheering, too, because his daughter certainly was. In fact, Dora's and Denny's hands were now waving in the air, joined above their heads in a giant upside down "V." And I noticed that when their arms dropped, they continued holding hands.

Up on the platform, Mayor Benton was practically glowing. "From now on, this woman gets anything she wants!" he shouted. And we all shouted, too, carrying on like it was the Fourth of July.

"Why don't we let Miss Millie get some rest?" Papa shouted over the din. "She's got a big day ahead of her tomorrow!"

Gradually, we began to disburse. Little Jack stayed on Noah's shoulders until we reached the Community Church on the corner. But I lingered back, watching Dora and Denny as they walked along ahead of us, hand in hand. Their arms were swinging back and forth in a rhythm that was totally unplanned and completely natural.

When had all this happened, I wondered? Or had it been happening all along, and I was the last one to know? And why would they let me know anyway? I was nothing to them. Nobody. Just good old Invisible Pidge Martin.

I guess I was so preoccupied with these thoughts that I didn't see Noah set Little Jack down. My brother must have been asking me something, because both he and Noah were staring at me now, waiting expectantly for an answer I didn't have.

Finally, Noah just shook his head like he didn't know what to do with me. "Are you all right?" he asked, and I remembered the other day at Sinkhole Lake, when he had asked me the same question. Was I all right? I didn't even know anymore.

When I didn't respond, Noah seemed hurt. Then angry. "You've been acting strange lately," he said.

"No, I haven't," I disagreed too quickly, immediately wishing I'd replied with something—anything—more congenial. I'd known Noah Blore ever since first grade and I'd never heard him say a cruel or critical word about anyone, least of all me. But now he was calling me "strange."

In anger, I fixed my attention on Denny and Dora again. They had stopped holding hands and were now staring at me, too, with the same questioning eyes as Noah's.

Little Jack swatted at my leg with his fist, and I turned my gaze downward.

"Let's go find Papa and Miss Millie," Little Jack said impatiently, and by the time I caught sight of Noah again, he was already on his way down Fielder Street, the back of his suit jacket looking too wrinkled and baggy for his narrow shoulders.

✻　✻　✻

We caught sight of Papa's truck, parked right in front of Chandler's Inn. The hotel, built in 1896, was the only place in town that offered clean beds and a free breakfast.

A small crowd was gathered outside, discussing the Rainmaker's arrival.

"Did you see how old she looks?"

"One foot in the grave, I'd say."

"And deaf as a post."

The two of us squeezed past them and entered the lobby, Little Jack in the lead. He spotted my father, with Miss Millie's bag, at the registration desk.

"Papa!" he yelled, charging across the wooden floor.

Millie herself was seated on a sagging couch near the elevator. Her eyes appeared round and endless behind her thinly framed glasses.

"Mornin', Miss Millie," I said, offering a hand to her. If she heard me, the woman showed no sign of it. I withdrew the hand, shoving it behind my back. "I'm Miriam Martin, Big Jack's daughter. But folks around here just call me Pidge."

Millie Boze's eyes finally focused on my face and she smiled benignly. "Nice to meet you, Midge."

I didn't correct her. What difference would it have made? The woman seemed confused and lost. Was this truly the miracle worker we had all been waiting for?

I sat next to her on the lumpy couch, folding both hands in my lap. "We're pretty excited about you making the rain for us and all," I said in my most polite voice.

She blinked rapidly. "Oh, I can't make rain, honey," she said pleasantly. "Not any more than I can make the sun rise or set every day."

I stared at her, not comprehending. "Then . . . how does it happen?"

"I don't know," she replied. When the woman observed my look of dismay she leaned closer and whispered. "Why does your hair grow and not your eyelashes? Why are some people right-handed and others left-handed?"

I shrugged helplessly, thinking that Miss Millie must be senile. Or completely mad.

She seemed to feel my frustration. "It's simply the way of things," she said, patting me on the shoulder. "There's no sense to any of it."

I looked into those round, moist eyes and saw only wonder. Could this woman really be enchanted, I thought? Or was she just lucky?

Papa and Little Jack were approaching, and I could not let them see my disappointment. If the Rainmaker's gifts should fail her this time around, there was nothing my father could do about it, was there? He had already paid for Miss Millie's trip and her accommodations. The fate of our town was now in the hands of this tiny wraith of a woman.

Little Jack pounced immediately. "When's it gonna rain?" he demanded, standing directly in front of the Rainmaker, nearly eye to eye.

Millie studied my brother seriously. "Soon," she answered, just as confident as you please.

Papa grinned proudly, as if to say, "See? What did I tell you?" I smiled back so hard, it made my teeth hurt.

"Now, let me show you to your room, Miss Millie," Papa said, offering her his arm. I followed the two of them to the elevator door, Little Jack bouncing behind me like a rubber ball.

"Ain't she something?" my brother said excitedly.

Was she? How could I know? Was Millie Boze magic or not? She'd said she couldn't produce rain, then promised its arrival. So where did this old woman's powers come from? Could she put an end to our town's drought merely by wishing it? Or did we have to do the wishing for her?

# 9

SUNDAY MORNING WAS CHURCH morning in Frostfree. But this Sunday was going to be a little bit different. This Sunday Papa was going to pick up Miss Millie from her hotel and bring her to church with us.

We couldn't all fit inside Papa's truck, of course, so Aunt Retta volunteered to stay at home. To be honest, I think she wanted to avoid the crowd that was sure to be in church this morning. Even those worshippers who only made it to Christmas and Easter services were bound to appear this particular Sunday, just to get an intimate peek at the Rainmaker.

"This way, I can prepare Sunday dinner in peace," my aunt added, wiping her forehead with a lacey handkerchief. It was already hot outside—nearly 90 degrees—and not yet even ten o'clock. I suspected that "peace" was not all my aunt was looking forward to, since the church was usually hotter than a steam bath in the summertime.

But I wasn't about to stay home and help my aunt, no matter how hot the church was. Magic or not, I wanted to be a part of all that excitement surrounding Miss Millie. And I wanted to see Denny and Noah, too, most especially Noah. I wanted to talk to him. But what would I say? Sorry I was mean to you? Sorry I've been acting strange? I had no explanation for my actions, or for my rudeness. So my apology wouldn't signify anything. *If* Noah even accepted it.

Maybe I'd blame it all on the drought.

❊   ❊   ❊

The preacher's sermon was mostly about miracles, and—in a roundabout way—rain. This had been Reverand Tanner's main topic, more or less, for the last four months. Today he talked about water drops on a penny, which didn't make a whole lot of sense to me, since water was what we were praying for in the first place. But I think this was his way of telling us that things take time.

I guess if you place little drops of water, one by one, on the surface of a penny, they will collect there in a bubble—without spilling over. Then finally, one last drop will suddenly do the trick. The bubble will burst, allowing the water to come spilling over the sides of the penny like a tiny waterfall. What we needed here in Frostfree, then, was that last drop of water. That last little miracle to let the rain come spilling out of the sky.

The miracle to which Reverend Tanner referred was Miss Millie, of course. That was no mystery to any of us. My eyes scanned the chapel, taking in the faces of all these people I had known my entire life. Each and every one of those faces was now turned toward Miss Millie, who sat smiling demurely, watching the preacher's mouth move, and not hearing a single word coming out of it.

Would she make the rain come, I wondered? And if she didn't, would our town just disappear? I had read about ghost towns in the West, entire cities that were abandoned when the gold or silver mines just dried up. The buildings and streets were still there, like shells left on a beach. But no one lived inside them, or walked on them. There was no reason for anyone to live there anymore. Would that happen to *us*? If the groves dried up, would we disappear, too?

I decided to pray extra hard when Reverend Tanner instructed us to bow our heads.

After the service was over, we all stood around outside, Papa introducing Miss Millie to people as if they didn't already know who she was. Little Jack was wrestling with Jimmy Tatum on the lawn, his Sunday suit picking up more grass than a lawn mower. Aunt Retta would be furious if she were here, but Papa didn't even seem to notice.

At the moment, he was presenting Miss Millie to Jenny Barton, the church organist who was so sweet on him. His left hand rested lightly on the small of Miss Jenny's back, and for some reason it made me feel good to know that Miss Millie hadn't heard any of the hymns the woman had performed earlier. I turned, feeling spiteful and not quite sure what to do about it.

That's when I caught a glimpse of Dr. Wheaton walking toward his car. Mrs. Wheaton trotted along briskly beside him with Dora lagging behind. Then Dora glanced back at the group gathered around Miss Millie, and I saw her give a quick wave to Denny, who stood leaning against an oak tree. He was grinning at her like a dopey dog, and I felt that old meanness from yesterday filling my chest and throat.

"So . . . how'd you like the sermon today?" came a voice from behind me.

It was Noah, dressed in the same suit and tie he had on yesterday. The tightness in my chest was now almost suffocating, and I couldn't respond.

He faced me, his expression unreadable. "Listen, do you want to talk or anything?"

I found my voice. "About what?"

"Well . . . about why you're so mad at me."

Mad at him? I wasn't mad at Noah. He was probably the nicest person I knew.

"I'm not mad at you," I said, my words coming out in a croak.

"You sure act like it sometimes."

"It's just the drought," I answered, not knowing what else to say.

"What's the drought got to do with it?" He took a step toward me. Noah's face was now so close, I could see tiny flecks of black in the green of his eyes. I wanted to touch him, but his cheeks were turning red, and I didn't know if he was angry or just getting too warm in his Sunday suit.

"I don't know," I answered quickly. "The drought makes me edgy, I guess."

I glanced away, the urge to touch Noah's face getting stronger, and I spied Miss Jenny Barton giving my father a kiss before she headed back into the church. It was just a peck really, on the side of one cheek. But the sight of it made something come up and out of my body, like a sigh. A memory from a long time ago, of my mother kissing my father just the same way. Where had that come from? I hadn't thought about my mother in weeks, not since Aunt

Retta had shown me the button from her shirt. The button which had belonged to Mama and which now belonged to my aunt.

All my mother's possessions had been given away it seemed, until there was nothing left of her. And now, Miss Jenny was kissing my father's cheek. My father's cheek, which had once belonged to my mother, too.

I felt tears welling up in my eyes, and I didn't want Noah to see them. He already thought I was strange enough.

"I have to go now," I said hoarsely. And I turned and fled, before he could ask me any more questions.

A group of reporters had now surrounded Miss Millie, and, spotting Papa and Little Jack, I joined the group gathered behind them. Unfortunately, Millie Boze wasn't an easy interview. The woman's hearing was so bad that the newspapermen had to write out their questions by hand. My father was patiently sorting through them, presenting the queries to her, one by one.

Where had Miss Millie gotten her special powers, one reporter wanted to know?

"Oh, from my brother," she answered sweetly. "He quit going on fishing trips because every time he headed for the lake, the skies opened up—and it poured."

"But how did his powers get passed on to you?" a second reporter scribbled for her.

Miss Millie's face grew serious. "Well . . . after my brother's death, I began to feel a peculiar power come over me. I can't explain it, but wherever I went it rained. All I had to do was pull out my umbrella and wait. The rain always came."

Most of the onlookers smiled uncomfortably, and a few of them were even rude enough to laugh. Miss Millie's story did sound mighty ridiculous, even to my ears. As much as I wanted to believe her, I just couldn't.

"Do you *pray* for rain?" wrote another reporter.

"Oh my, no!" exclaimed Miss Millie. "I am a good Christian, but I don't need to pray for changes in the weather." Then she gave the man a sly grin. "No incantations, rain dances, or secret potions, either. I just have the power to bring rain; never could explain it."

This was followed by genuine laughter from the crowd. At least we were laughing *with* Miss Millie now, but I still think a number of the spectators had lost all hope in their miracle. Millie Boze was a sweet old lady who had journeyed here all the way from Oxford, Mississippi. But it didn't seem likely that rain would follow her to Frostfree, or anywhere else for that matter.

"If you fail to bring rain to Frostfree in the next forty-eight hours, do you intend to return the money?" read another note. It wasn't signed, but I figured the question just had to be from Mr. Hank Giles, owner of the sunken B & B Grocery Store— and Dr. Wheaton's latest ally. I was pretty sure Doc Wheaton would have asked the question himself, if he'd had the nerve to stick around.

To my surprise, Miss Millie merely appeared puzzled. "Why, no," she said simply. "I need that money to get back to Mississippi. Besides, I have never failed."

That seemed to stop the note passing. No one knew what to ask this woman, after such a bold declaration. My father held up his hand to signal that the interview had come to an end.

"Miss Millie is probably very tired," he announced, "and she needs her rest for the rainmaking ceremony this afternoon."

Rainmaking ceremony? This was the first I'd heard of such a thing. But then, everything about Miss Millie's visit had become a ceremony, hadn't it?

Papa took the old woman's elbow and led her to our truck. Little Jack even surprised us all by running ahead and opening the door for her. My brother and I helped her into the backseat, and Papa began to pull away when there was a loud thump on the window.

A photographer from the local paper was waving a camera at us, jogging alongside the car and signaling for Miss Millie to roll down the back window. She began to reach for the handle when Papa slowed the car to a stop and looked back at her.

"You don't have to do this, Miss Millie," he said loudly, clearly annoyed with the persistent cameraman.

"I don't mind," she said sweetly, "if it makes the man happy."

Millie Boze rolled down the window and faced the camera, her expression now serious and purposeful, that of a Rainmaker about to do her job. The photographer fiddled with his camera for a few minutes, as the woman waited patiently for him to adjust his settings and lenses. Finally, he pressed a button, which made the camera's bulb practically explode in Miss Millie's face.

"Thanks, lady!" he yelled, running back toward the church lawn and his fellow newspapermen. He was waving the camera over his head like a trophy.

Papa started up the car again, leaving a cyclone of dust behind us.

"I'm sorry you had to put up with that, Miss Millie," he said angrily.

I couldn't be sure if she heard his words or not, but the Rainmaker's eyes danced wickedly in her wrinkled face. "Oh, I've seen it all before, dearie," she said calmly.

# 10

Dinner at noon was rushed and
wordless. Even Little Jack was quiet, for once. All of
us just wanted to eat as hastily as possible, so we
wouldn't miss a single minute of Miss Millie's "Rain
Ceremony" this afternoon. Aunt Retta fussed about
our table manners, but I could tell she was excited,
too. Her hair was now neatly tucked into a bun, and
she had purchased a brand-new hat with pink
ribbons for the occasion.

Millie Boze was scheduled to make an appearance

on the banks of Palmer Lake around 2:00. Papa had chosen this spot because it was wide open to the elements and seemed the perfect location to solicit rain. Palmer Lake was also a popular picnic spot, and its shores provided plenty of dead grass for the onlookers, who planned to sit themselves down on it while Miss Millie charmed rain out of the sky.

Cars and trucks were parked all around the lake's perimeter, and a number of them began honking their horns as we approached the waterfront. In order to accommodate Miss Millie, Little Jack had submitted to sitting in Retta's lap for the trip over, but he was too excited to grumble about it.

"This here's Palmer Lake," he was explaining to Miss Millie. "It's usually lots deeper, but the water level's down—on account of the drought."

Miss Millie nodded kindly at him. I'm sure she hadn't heard a word he'd said. At her feet lay her special "rainmaking" supplies: a quilt, a newspaper, and a box of fresh strawberries. That was it. I was surely having my doubts about this woman's abilities, and I could tell Aunt Retta was, too. She kept plucking at the skirt of her dress and rearranging her hat. And every few minutes or so, she would sneak fretful glances at Miss Millie in the backseat.

Little Jack was as optimistic as ever, of course. This was a great adventure, and he was right in the middle of it.

"Will it be raining by tonight, do you think?" he asked Millie.

The woman merely smiled and gazed out the window at the approaching lake.

"Shush, Little Jack," I admonished. "I'm sure Miss Millie needs to concentrate right now."

"Aw, shoot. She's just gawkin' out the window," he pouted, but he stopped pestering her.

Papa pulled up next to Jeff Tatum's red pickup truck, and we all piled out. The spectators who were gathered around the shore sat eerily still, like trees just before a hurricane. No one said a word as Miss Millie spread her quilt upon the grass, setting herself down next to the newspaper and her strawberries. Serenely, she began reading the paper and munching on the strawberries.

Was this what it was like to witness a miracle, I thought? Everyone standing around, holding their breaths? When would it actually happen? And when would we *know* it had happened?

I caught sight of Miss Jenny Barton making her way toward us, and I remembered the kiss from this morning. That woman had some nerve, I thought, chasing after Papa while he was busy supervising a miracle. Although I had to admit his job wasn't looking too strenuous at the moment.

Miss Jenny plopped herself down, right next to Papa and Little Jack. "Hey, you two," she said, with a bright smile. I noticed she had lipstick on her teeth.

Little Jack regarded her with scant interest. Aunt Retta scooted over to make room for her on our blanket, but Miss Barton squeezed in close to Papa.

"Nice day out," my father commented to Miss Jenny.

Who was he fooling? It was hotter'n blazes out here.

Miss Jenny leaned forward, peering around my father. "Hey, Pidge. When are y'all going to start taking piano lessons?"

When hell freezes over, I thought. "Oh, I don't know. I've been pretty busy this summer," I answered. Papa's lips emitted a low whistle, which said I'd been doing absolutely *nothing* all summer long. Retta added her own little snort. I paid them no mind.

Meanwhile, folks around the lake began to get restless, watching Miss Millie read her newspaper. I think they were expecting something a little more momentous, or at least more entertaining. This was downright boring.

Miss Millie chomped on another strawberry. She turned a page of her newspaper. Aunt Retta coughed. Papa cleared his throat.

"When's the rain gonna come?" Little Jack complained.

Papa ran a hand over the blond mop on Little

Jack's head. "Not right away," he said gently. "Miracles take time, you know."

My brother stared out over the lake. "Tell me somethin' I don't already know," he said angrily. Little Jack wasn't the most patient person in the world.

Then, without warning, Papa stood. He hoisted my brother into the air and spun him around a few times. "Good things come to those who wait," he said, after setting Little Jack back down on the blanket. "Didn't anyone ever tell you that?"

"Not so's I'd remember it," Little Jack snapped.

Miss Jenny and Retta shared a laugh together.

"Why, miracles happen every day, Little Jack," Miss Jenny told him. "Sometimes they're so tiny, you don't even realize they've happened. I'll bet you've seen lots of them."

"Like when?" he said, intrigued.

"Well . . . like one day you learned how to read, didn't you? But do you remember when? Can you tell me the exact moment you suddenly knew you could read?"

Little Jack didn't read all that well *now*, to tell the truth. But I didn't expect Miss Jenny to know that.

"Or small acts of kindness," Miss Jenny went on. "A favor done without asking, a touch when you're feeling ill, a smile when you're feeling sad."

"A kiss," I added, staring her straight in the eye.

"Yes. That, too," she said, her cheeks reddening before she looked away. I glanced over at Papa and noticed that his face was also flushed now, clear down his neck and into the collar of his dress shirt.

I sensed a stirring among the crowd and saw that Miss Millie was starting to get up from her blanket. The Rainmaker's vigil had come to an end, it seemed, with very little fanfare. But how had she known she was finished?

Papa stepped briskly over to Miss Millie, helping her up. She handed him her newspaper and empty strawberry box.

"Well . . . that should do the trick," she said to him, as if she had actually accomplished something.

I watched my aunt, who was fiddling with the ribbons on her hat like they were live snakes. None of us knew exactly what to say. None of us except Little Jack, that is.

"So. When's the rain gonna come?" he asked again, loud enough not only for Miss Millie, but for half of Frostfree to hear.

"In a day or two," she replied calmly, folding her quilt in half and then in half again. Since my father's hands were full, I took it from her. The quilt didn't feel special at all. It was just a plain old bed cover, with the usual accumulation of stains and loose threads.

I looked up at the sky, blue and cloudless and

hazy with heat. The same old sky, I thought. The same old heat. And I could feel a small empty hole inside me begin to widen, just above my stomach.

We loaded ourselves into the truck and pulled out onto the highway, cars lining up neatly behind us like mourners in a funeral procession. For the first time, I noticed Mr. Blore's green Chevy among them and wondered if Noah was inside. Had he been there to witness Miss Millie's "miracle"? Just two days ago, I would have laughed with him about her quilt and her strawberries, but now I felt awkward around him. Strange. Wasn't that what Noah himself had said about me? *You've been acting strange lately.*

The air inside Papa's truck felt close and damp. I suddenly had the intense urge to roll down a window and throw my head out, letting the fresh air course through my hair like long breathing fingers. But as I reached across Miss Millie for the window handle, I saw that her face was now tilted, chin upward, her head thrown back over the seat. The woman's mouth had fallen open, and her glasses hung slightly askew.

The miraculous Rainmaker had fallen asleep.

✳   ✳   ✳

That evening I sat on my bed and went through the box of my mother's belongings. It had been years since I'd sorted through the keys and jewelry, draped Mama's scarves over my arms and around my neck. And the objects felt foreign to me now, as if they belonged to a stranger. I thought about the kiss Miss Jenny had given my father this morning, and about the Rainmaker's blanket, which had felt so ordinary and insignificant in my hands. So expendable. The emptiness I'd experienced this afternoon swelled, until I had to clutch my stomach, unable to hold back tears I hadn't even known were there.

I sobbed and sobbed, sucking in long hollow breaths of air. It felt as if my chest were about to split wide open—and the worst part of it was I didn't know why. I just kept on crying, but it didn't make me feel any better.

After a time, the room darkened. A shadow fell across one side of my bed, and I knew it was Papa. I felt his weight upon the mattress before I saw his hand beside me on the quilt. The hand was big and strong, veined and freckled from years of tending oranges in the Florida sun. But it was gentle and fair, too, and had always comforted me when nothing else could.

Papa reached into the box, fingering a necklace and then a silver brooch. Finally, he drew a tiny key out of the jumble. It was no bigger than a safety pin.

He rolled the key around and around in his

hand. "This is the key to your mother's diary," he said quietly.

I sat up, trying to process this information. Mama had owned a diary? Why hadn't Papa ever told me? Did he still have it? And if he did, why hadn't I been allowed to read it?

Papa sighed, as if seeing into my mind. "Sometimes, Pidge," he said, "there are things that people just shouldn't have to know."

Things about my mother, I wondered? But of course, that was exactly what he was trying to tell me. There were things I could never know about my mother. But why? Who was he to decide what I should or should not know? Suddenly, I wanted to tell my father about the hollow feeling in my stomach, about my own mother being a stranger to me. What could be worse than not knowing anything about her at all?

I glimpsed a sliver of moon, just visible through the corner of my window. And I had a flash of memory, gone almost as quickly as it had appeared. My mother coming into my room . . . her breath on my cheek . . . her fingers in the dark.

"Mama left us, didn't she?" I said.

Papa gazed out the window, too, and he slipped an arm around me. "It wasn't her fault, Pidge. I guess maybe I wanted her to get better too much. Wanted it so bad, I started to believe in it." Then he handed the tiny key to me and left the room.

When he returned, my father held a square-shaped book in his hand. It was flat and blue, its cover blank and disappointingly ordinary.

Papa placed the book on my bed. "The doctors told her to write in this," he said. "I've never read any of it."

I was afraid to touch it, and I almost hoped he wouldn't answer my next question.

"Do you *want* me to read it?"

He smoothed the hair from my face and planted a delicate kiss on my cheek, like the one Miss Jenny had given him this morning. "I just want you to be happy, darlin'."

After he left, I sat on my bed, brooding for a long time. I listened to the sounds of Aunt Retta banging dishes around in preparation for supper, and my papa's slow easy laugh as he teased Little Jack into setting the table.

Then I began to read.

# 11

WHO KNOWS WHEN SOMEBODY'S LIFE starts to go wrong? Was there one particular day when my mother knew for certain things would never get better? Were there any signs that my father could have recognized—and what would he have done about them if he'd seen them? Maybe Papa had just done what he thought was right.

Mama's diary was a jumble of words and phrases. Nothing connected, and none of it made sense. Occasionally, she would scribble in dates or days of the week, but I'm not even sure if she knew what day it was most of the time. *I hate it here. I just want to die. Why won't he let me come home?*

She was in a hospital. I had figured that much out. And she blamed my father for keeping her there. But Mama *had* come home, at least once. This wasn't in her diary, but I knew it was true because I had felt her there in my room. On the night she'd died. My mother had come back to say good-bye to me.

Had my father allowed her to return home? Or had my mother simply left the hospital on her own? Papa must have known that she would rather die than go back. Maybe, in the end, he'd decided home would be best. Maybe he really believed Mama would get better all by herself. Or, maybe he knew she wouldn't.

But now I had put all these "maybe's" together— and it frightened me. Seven years ago, my mother had been mentally ill, and she'd wanted to die. And my father had let it happen. Maybe not intentionally, but it had happened. *Sometimes there are things that people just shouldn't have to know,* he'd said to me. Was he talking about Mama, or about himself? Could her diary tell me?

But this diary wasn't my mother. It was just a bunch of words. Tangled thoughts from a woman who was too removed from life to live it anymore. I saw now that I would never know Mama at all. Not from this book of hers, anyway.

I wanted to cry again, knew that I probably should. But now I could not. Too many things were pulling at my mind, sucking me down. It felt as if I were moving underwater, wildly pushing and kicking to break free from crosscurrents I couldn't even see. Fighting to breathe.

I was angry at my mother for doing this to me. For never letting me know her, and for leaving Little Jack with nothing but a ghost to remember. Worse, I was mad at Papa for allowing all of it to go wrong. I'd always thought my father was so strong, so . . . right. But now he was as much a stranger to me as Mama had been. It was like he'd been living a whole different life, separate from me and Little Jack. My father had kept secrets from us, and I suddenly felt sick.

More important than that, I felt betrayed. This was a horrible thing to know, and I didn't want it. I wished Papa had never shown me that awful diary, because now I would have to live with his secret, like some horrible wart I could never get rid of. Was that how he felt? Was he angry, too? Or just terribly sad?

While I sat there, still unable to cry, I heard footsteps coming up the stairs, and I quickly stashed Mama's book under my pillow. Little Jack appeared in the doorway, an angry scowl on his face.

"Aunt Retta says supper is ready and y'all better get down to the table before the food gets cold." Then he noticed the box on my bed. "What's that?"

"Some things of Mama's. Pins and jewelry and stuff."

Little Jack jumped up onto the bed to examine the contents more closely. He picked up a bracelet from the box and carefully slipped it onto his skinny little arm. I think he was trying to see how it was to be Mama, to imagine how something of hers might feel against his body, close to his skin.

The bracelet rolled off his wrist, of course, like running water. But he picked it right back up again, to try it on a second time. And as I watched him, I began to think that *this* might be my mother. Not some diary full of piled-up words. Mama's box of odds and ends was the closest I would ever get to her, the last small things she could give to me. Or to Little Jack.

For some reason, this made me think about Reverend Tanner's sermon this morning. About how water collects on the surface of a penny, and then that one last drop finally makes it spill over. Like a tiny waterfall. And as I live and breathe, that was when I finally started to cry.

Silent tears trickled down my face, a few of them landing on the bedspread, and it took a while before Little Jack even noticed I was weeping. He dropped the bracelet, like it was on fire.

"Pidge?" he said, sounding scared. "Are you all right?"

If one more person asked me that question, I thought I might scream. But I smiled through my tears and mussed up his hair. Then I hugged him, real hard.

My brother squirmed out from under my grasp. "Stop that, y'hear?" he said angrily. But he didn't climb down off the bed.

I held the bracelet out to him. "Wanna try it on again?" I asked.

He backed away warily. "You gonna start crying again?"

I shook my head no, and he snatched the bracelet before I could change my mind.

Up until now, I had always kept Mama's box hidden, stashed under my bed like a secret I could let out only one little bit at a time. But I wanted to share it now, let my brother own some of it, too.

"You can help yourself to Mama's things any time you want," I told him. "I'll keep the box on my desk."

Little Jack eyed me suspiciously, like there must be some sort of catch. "Can I keep some of it?"

I wasn't sure I wanted to go that far, but I knew it was unfair of me to horde Mama's jewelry all to myself. "Sure," I said. "You can even give that bracelet to your girlfriend some day."

My brother actually blushed before butting his head into my stomach.

"Go jump in a lake," he said, but he was smiling.

We both got up from the bed, and I placed Mama's box on top of my desk. Right out there in the open, where anyone could see it.

Then Little Jack and I went downstairs for supper.

❊　❊　❊

Aunt Retta kept aiming glances at Papa while we ate. She even patted my hand once, after passing me the mashed potatoes. That was out of the ordinary for her. My aunt wasn't given to touching or hugging, any more than Little Jack was. But I knew she was worried about me, about the knowledge I now carried—like an extra arm or leg. So I tried to act normal at the dinner table, as much for her sake as for Papa's.

"Little Jack," Retta said, as she was clearing the dishes, "why don't you help me wash up, so your papa and Pidge can go sit outside on the porch?"

My brother gave her a look like he'd just swallowed something rotten. "Why would they want to do that? Ain't nothing but mosquitoes out there!"

Papa tipped his chair back, smiling over at me. "How about it, Pidge? I could sure use some company."

I nodded, not knowing what to say. Little Jack stomped off to the sink, angrier than a bear before breakfast. He was jealous that Papa hadn't asked *him* to join us on the porch.

"You can come out too, Little Jack," Papa said, "soon as the dishes are done."

My brother grunted, his back still to us. Then Aunt Retta leaned down to whisper something in his ear, and I heard him giggle.

Papa and I stepped out onto the porch, each of us sitting in one of the rockers under the window. We rocked wordlessly for a while, the creaking of the chairs mingling with the sounds of the crickets and the cicadas, until I couldn't decide which was complaining loudest. My heart was beating faster than a scared rabbit's, but I just had to ask my father one thing.

"Papa?" I whispered into the breathless evening, "How did Mama die?"

His rocker stopped, and he shifted his body, placing an ankle on top of one knee.

"Don't know exactly. Pills, I reckon. At least, that's what the doctors said. They think it was an accident."

I swallowed real hard. "Do *you* think it was an accident?"

"Had to be," he said without hesitation. "She never would have left us on purpose."

"Was Mama . . . here when it happened?"

"No, darlin'. I'd already sent her on back to the hospital."

Tears burned at the back of my eyes, as I thought

about the words in Mama's diary. She had hated that hospital. "But why?" I asked. "Why did she have to go back?"

Papa hissed softly through his teeth. He started rocking again, real slow. "I thought she could be happy here, Pidge. Thought maybe having her come home to you and me and Little Jack might be enough. But it wasn't."

"Did the doctors know what was wrong with her?"

"Depression. That's what they said, anyway. Went through a bad spell after you were born, but she got over it. I guess it was a whole lot worse after Little Jack, though." He leaned forward, resting both elbows on his knees. "Funny thing, ain't it? Nothing made her happier than being with you two kids, so why would having babies make her so sad?"

I couldn't come up with an answer to that, but I knew from reading Mama's diary that nothing about her illness made sense. "I think she was just confused," I said, and Papa smiled at me gratefully.

"She was that," he said. "And stubborn. Just wanted to come home and be with you and Little Jack, no matter what those doctors were telling her. Iris was a strong-willed, opinionated woman." He grinned at me, the moonlight showing off the white of his teeth from the darkness of his tanned, lined face. "Sort of runs in the family."

I grinned back at him. I could hear my brother laughing in the kitchen and knew he'd be out here soon to pester us. Him and the mosquitoes. I didn't know which was worse.

"When will you tell Little Jack?" I asked, wondering if my brother could ever understand the reasons behind Mama's death. I wasn't even sure that Papa understood them. And I certainly knew that I didn't.

Papa said, "When he's ready, I guess." Not much of an answer, I thought.

"But when will *that* be?" I insisted.

Papa laughed. "See what I mean about stubborn women in this family?" But when I didn't answer, he grew serious again. "All right, Pidge. How about if you and I decide together? When we think the time is right."

"But how will we know?"

Papa rocked back and forth, back and forth. "Oh, if I know Little Jack, he'll *let* us know."

I remembered how my father had found me this afternoon, picking through Mama's box of trinkets on the bed and crying as if my heart had broken. "The way I did?"

But before Papa could reply, Little Jack came crashing through the door. He ran across the porch, pitching himself onto Papa's lap. Aunt Retta followed, dragging a couple of kitchen chairs with her. She sat heavily in one, then began fanning her face with a damp dishtowel.

"Phew! Feels a bit more humid than *usual* tonight," she said breathily.

I sat up straight in my rocking chair. Could Aunt Retta be right? Was it really more humid this evening? Out of habit, I looked up overhead, hoping to see rain clouds. All I got was a sky full of stars.

My father tickled Little Jack's stomach, and my brother wiggled on his lap like a turtle turned upside down.

"Must mean rain is on the way," Papa said to Retta, and Little Jack instantly sprang up, too.

"Of course rain is on the way," he said, as if my father didn't have the brains he was born with. "In a day or two. Miss Millie said so."

Papa and Aunt Retta chuckled, and my father added, "Well, if Miss Millie said so, then it must be so."

Little Jack grinned triumphantly. "Now, tell me somethin' I don't already know," he crowed.

But none of us did.

# 12

MISS MILLIE BOZE LEFT FROSTFREE THE following morning. Her departure took place without any frills or fuss, much like Miss Millie herself.

A small crowd was assembled at the train station to see her off, but enthusiasm had cooled considerably since the Rainmaker's arrival two days ago. For one thing, there still wasn't a cloud in the sky. The air pressed down on us, hot and damp, so thick it felt like you could run a fork through it. For another, Miss Millie's uninspired performance yesterday afternoon hadn't impressed anybody. The woman was too sweet to chase out of town. Still, no one wanted to give her much of a send-off, either.

We drove Miss Millie to the station: just Papa, Little Jack, and me. Aunt Retta was suffering from swollen joints again and had chosen to spend the morning in bed. At least that was the excuse she had given. But I think she was a bit disappointed in the Rainmaker's lack of results so far. For a while, my aunt had allowed herself to get caught up in the magic. And now she felt like a fool, letting herself get carried away like that. Shoot, I guess we all felt a little foolish.

All except Papa, that is. He smiled and waved at the handful of onlookers gathered at the train station, as he gently led Miss Millie onto the platform. I wasn't feeling at all congenial myself. My thoughts were still tangled around the words I'd read in Mama's diary last night. And watching Papa up there now with Miss Millie only made me feel more confused. One minute I'd be angry about what happened to my mother, and the next minute I'd feel this enormous tide of sadness envelop me like a roiling black thundercloud.

Seeing Denny and Noah didn't help my mood any, either. They were sitting on a bench near the end of the platform, hands in pockets and legs outstretched. At the moment, I didn't want to talk to either one of them. Lately, it seemed like everybody and everything in Frostfree was aggravating me. And that included Little Jack.

"Hey, there's Denny and Noah!" he shouted, pointing at them as if I didn't have eyes in my own head. "Let's go over and see 'em."

"I can see them just fine from right here," I said prissily.

An exasperated Little Jack shook his head and then bolted across the platform to talk with the boys himself. I gratefully ignored all three of them.

"Here's your train ticket back home, Miss Millie," Papa was saying. He handed her a large white envelope, and she took it from him with a slight bob of her head. Millie appeared especially fragile this morning, as if her arm might break from the weight of that one slim ticket in her hand. Maybe her "rainmaking" had taken more out of her than I had assumed. After all, being sixty-seven years old was hard enough without adding rain vigils and 98-degree weather on top of it.

Papa shook her frail little hand, then dropped it gently. She turned to me.

"It was very nice meeting you, Miriam," Miss Millie said, and it took a moment to register that she was addressing *me*. She glanced down the length of the platform, adding, "And that mischievous little brother of yours, too."

We heard the double whistle and turned our bodies south, in anticipation of the train's arrival. I noticed that Noah and Denny were now standing straight up on the bench. They cheered and hollered when the train came into view, Little Jack whooping it up from on top of Noah's shoulders. Now I was angry that I wasn't waiting over there with them, but what had I expected? A written invitation?

Papa helped Miss Millie onto the train, handing the woman's one small bag to the conductor. Then we all waved, as the train made its way through the station, heading up north to Georgia, and Alabama and Mississippi.

Papa stood beside me, and without saying a word he put an arm around me, pulling my body close into his side. It felt right, standing there together. And we watched the thin plume of black smoke snake its way upward, long after the small crowd had dispersed and the train had disappeared from view.

Little Jack ran over to us, Noah and Denny following close behind.

"When's it gonna rain?" Little Jack demanded, for about the hundredth time in the last twenty-four hours.

Papa peered up at the blue, cloudless haze. "Not today, I'm afraid."

"Do you think Miss Millie's magic will really

work, Mr. Martin?" Noah came right out and asked, and my throat went suddenly tight. I stared at my father, *willing* him to say yes. If my father didn't believe in the Rainmaker, then how could the rest of us believe in her? But Papa had believed my mother would get better, too. And she hadn't.

Papa regarded Noah, his mouth easing itself into a warm, molasses smile.

"Well, outguessing God sort of limits your wishes, now don't it?" he said.

This was not the answer Noah and Denny had wanted to hear. Their expressions turned wary, as if my father actually might be the swindler Doc Wheaton had pronounced him to be. Little Jack looked plain old disgusted. But I thought I knew what Papa meant.

Once, when I was around nine or ten, I'd got it into my head that Papa was building me a rocking horse out in the barn—for my birthday. I wished for it so hard that I began seeking hidden clues to prove I was right. *If Papa takes a hammer into the barn, then he's working on that rocking horse. If Papa buys nails in town tomorrow, then they're for my rocking horse.*

By the time my birthday came around, I was so set on that horse that I nearly died of disappointment when my father carried in the dollhouse he'd been working on for months. It took three days before I'd handle the miniature tables and chairs, or even touch the hand-carved dolls of me and Little Jack.

Finally, Aunt Retta pulled me aside and gave me a good talking-to.

"What's wrong with you, Pidge? Is there something else you were wanting? The crown jewels, maybe? Or possibly a big old cattle ranch?"

And it was then that I realized I hadn't really wanted the rocking horse at all. I had just wanted to be right. I'd been so busy expecting the horse, that I'd completely missed out on the joy of receiving the dollhouse. And then it was too late for me to feel anything. I'd put all my hopes into something that wasn't even real.

But Papa had put all his hopes—and money—into Miss Millie, hadn't he? What would happen if he was wrong about her, too?

Denny grumbled, kicking a stone out across the railroad tracks with the toe of his shoe. "Don't seem to be much around here to hope for *except* rain," he said, and my father squinted up at the sky again, tightening his grip on my shoulders.

"Didn't say not to hope," Papa said quietly. "But don't start counting on it."

We heard the crunch of tires on gravel and turned to see Dr. Wheaton's silver gray Packard pull into the station and glide to a stop. Out stepped

Dora and her father, along with Mrs. Wheaton in a flowery hat and pointy shoes.

"Mornin', Big Jack," Dr. Wheaton boomed, ignoring the rest of us.

"Win," replied Papa, with a slight nod of his head. Then he added, "Mrs. Wheaton, Miss Wheaton." The two men stood facing each other, the awkwardness between them even thicker than the air.

"Did we miss Miss Millie's send-off?" Dora asked, a little too brightly. She must have known they had, considering there were only five of us left at the station. But for once I was grateful that Dora had spoken up. She'd probably wanted to break the silence, and her question had done just that.

"Miss Millie left about twenty minutes ago," Denny said, grinning at Dora with that dopey-dog look of his. And there she stood, grinning right back. I felt like an outsider—or worse—an intruder. I was pretty sure Noah did, too.

Little Jack, as usual, was oblivious. "Hey, Dora," he said, gaping at her with undisguised adoration. What was it about Dora Wheaton and boys? That girl had a pull stronger than the earth's gravity.

"Hey, Little Jack," she said to him, as sweet as could be.

Mr. Wheaton cleared his throat. "I'd like to talk to you, Big Jack," he said to my father. Then, as if suddenly remembering that the rest of us were here, too, he reached into his pocket and pulled out a shiny new quarter.

"Dora," he said brightly, "why don't y'all go down to Mr. Giles's new store and get yourselves some peppermint sticks?"

I knew the "y'all" probably included Little Jack and me, but something tugged at me to stay here and find out what Dr. Wheaton really wanted with my father. What was so important that he needed to confront Papa here at the station? And why had he and his wife made sure that Millie was on that train before coming to meet with him?

Papa gave my elbow a light squeeze. "You go on, now," he said. "I'll see you at home."

I left reluctantly, hanging back a little from the rest of them as we headed south on Fielder Street. Mr. Giles had opened a temporary market on the corner opposite the Community Church, while his brand-new grocery store was under construction a few blocks away. The market was nothing more than a tent, really. But Mr. and Mrs. Giles stocked fresh fruit and vegetables from out of the state, along with a few dry goods—and, of course, candy.

Dora and Denny examined the candy jar, eventually picking out the two longest peppermint sticks. Little Jack and Noah both chose licorice, but I just couldn't decide. Everything made my mouth water, and yet I wasn't hungry. Maybe the heat was spoiling my appetite.

"Mornin', Pidge." It was Mrs. Giles, smiling at me from over the top of the wooden counter. "Miss Millie make it off all right this morning?"

"Yes, ma'am," I replied, although I didn't think Mrs. Giles cared for the Rainmaker any more than Doc Wheaton did. She was just being sociable. "I guess I'll have a couple of those lemon drops, please."

Mrs. Giles handed me the candies, and Dora paid for our purchases. Then we all walked across the street to the Community Church, where we could sit in the shade and slurp noisily.

Denny and Dora held hands as they traded licks on their candy sticks. The very idea make me sick, and I turned my back on them.

"What do you think Doc Wheaton wanted?" Noah asked. He had snuck up on me again, without my noticing.

I shrugged, not especially interested anymore. "Wish I knew."

"Maybe he's changed his mind about the Rainmaker."

I scanned the sky, searching for rain clouds. Seems I'd been doing that a lot lately. "Not likely," I replied.

Noah stood on the church steps with me awhile

longer, taking an occasional nibble on his licorice stick. He was never one to say much, but he seemed comfortable with that. And I felt comfortable standing here next to him, saying nothing right back.

Then Little Jack ran over and grabbed his hand. "Swing me around, Noah!" he begged.

Noah looked at me.

"Go ahead," I said, and the two of them charged out across the lawn.

I sat on the steps, watching them and remembering the day at Sinkhole Lake when Denny had swung Dora around on his shoulders. Why couldn't I be as comfortable around boys as Dora seemed to be? Did I need to giggle and flirt to get them to notice me? If so, I was in big trouble because I had no idea how to do any of that nonsense.

I could hear Dora giggling right now, as a matter of fact. She and Denny must have sneaked around the corner of the building to the choir room entrance. I didn't think I could stand much more of their hand-holding and candy-sharing, so I was prepared to join Noah and my brother on the lawn when I heard my name.

Denny and Dora were talking about *me*? I crept a little closer to the corner of the church, not wanting to be heard. Shamelessly, I listened to every word.

"Oh, she's crazy about Noah. Can't you tell?" Giggle, giggle.

"You're the one who's crazy," Denny was whispering. "Pidge is meaner to Noah than a dog on a scent. Shoot, she's mean to everybody."

"That's the way girls are," Dora informed him. This was news to me. "She just doesn't want Noah to *know* that she likes him."

"Wait a minute. She likes him, so she's mean to him? Sounds like *she's* the one who's crazy then."

"Shhhh . . . that's not very nice, considering . . ."

"Considering what?"

"Considering that her own mama was crazy, too, you know. Died under *very* mysterious circumstances, is what I heard."

"*What???*"

"Well, that's what my mama says . . ."

I couldn't listen to this anymore. My Aunt Retta was right. Eavesdroppers never heard anything they wanted to hear. How could Dora even *dare* to tell Denny something like this? Something so personal? So private? As if a person's death were something to gossip about?

Without thinking, I charged around the corner, facing them both. I was glad to see the perpetual smirk finally wiped off Denny's face. As for Dora, she stared at me open-mouthed, her complexion pale.

"You think your mama knows every little thing?" I shouted, not caring now *who* heard me. "Well, she doesn't!"

Dora eventually found her voice. "I didn't say my mama knows everything," she answered meekly. But I was in no mood to listen to Dora Wheaton anymore. She'd said enough.

"For your information, my mother was *not* crazy. She was . . . mentally ill. And how she died is none of your business!"

"Pidge, I'm sorry—"

"You got no right, talking about things you know nothing about," I said, the words spilling out of my mouth like water from an overturned bucket. I felt the tears starting, and I didn't want to cry. Not in front of Dora. I wanted to hurt her, but I didn't know how. I was out of her league in the hurting department.

Dora's fingers plucked at her fancy dress. "I'm sorry," she said again, weakly.

I couldn't forgive her, so there didn't seem to be anything left to say. It was time to gather up my brother and go on home. But when I turned around, I saw Noah and Little Jack, still standing on the lawn in front of the church. Noah was holding on tight to my brother's hand. Little Jack's eyes were as shiny and round as two brand-new nickels.

Neither one of them had missed a thing.

# 13

LITTLE JACK TOOK OFF FIRST, around the back of the church and into the woods. Noah immediately lit out after him, with me following right behind. My brother could run fast for such a skinny little thing, and before long Noah had lost sight of the tiny silhouette darting through the trees.

He stopped to catch his breath, head down, hands on his knees. I came up beside him, the sound of dried leaves crunching underneath my shoes.

"It's okay, Noah," I said. "He's just running on home anyway."

"You sure?" he gasped, not even bothering to lift his head.

"Where else would he go?"

We stood there, not speaking. I watched a squirrel leap from an overhanging branch, and I remembered that day Little Jack and I had walked through the woods together to get him some new shoes. On that particular morning, he'd wanted to be a baseball player. Or was it a movie star? Well, whatever it was, he'd been happy. So cocky and full of himself. And I'd wanted to put him in his place. A seven-year-old. As if a kid that little even had a *place* to begin with.

Noah finally stood up. Sweat dripped along the sides of his face and down his neck. He grinned at me. "Fast little cuss, ain't he?"

I laughed. "Faster than a rabbit in the wind, Papa says."

Before long the two of us left the woods and started down the road out of town, into orange grove country. It was land that Noah and I knew well. Hadn't known any other, when it came to that. One farm just sort of ran into the next. And if a citrus grove was ever in any trouble, folks from miles around would chip in to help. Didn't matter who owned what, or if a man could even pay you back. The oranges were the only thing that mattered. And that meant they had to have water. Not only

Papa's oranges, or Noah's oranges, or Mr. Tatum's oranges. But everybody's oranges.

I thought about the "Depression" our country was going through now, how everyone was pitching in and working and saving, just trying to get by. But it seemed like the drought here was something apart from all of that. Like maybe Frostfree was this sad, dried-up little place that everyone else had completely forgotten about. And maybe the rain had just forgotten about us, too.

I shuffled along beside Noah, conscious of him next to me, and knowing that he wanted to ask about my mother. But then he surprised me.

"You don't like Dora much, do you?" he said.

I searched for the right words to say, then came up with one. "No."

He laughed. "Sure don't beat around the bush now, do you?"

I shrugged. "You asked."

He put his hands in his pockets and looked off down the road. "Sometimes I don't much like her, either," he admitted. "But I think she's tryin'."

I came to a halt, staring at him. "Trying what?"

"To fit in."

I snorted and continued walking. How hard was it to fit in with a bunch of country farmers? We didn't put on airs like she did. Or talk about people behind their backs. And we certainly didn't throw our money around town, the way her father did.

Noah's voice came out high and strained. "You should just try to get along with her, Pidge. That's all I'm saying."

I stared at the dusty road beneath my feet. Noah didn't understand. He had no idea how awkward I felt around Dora, how angry I was about what she'd just told Denny.

"Oh, really," I said. "And why should I do that?"

"Because she's here, whether you like it or not. Dora's one of us now."

My lips began to tremble, and I bit down hard on them to make the quivering stop. "You're just saying that because Denny likes her," I retorted.

"Awww, Pidge," he said quietly, then fell silent.

We had come to the end of our drive. Up ahead, I could see our house in miniature, with its wooden porch and the oak tree growing, like a gnarled arm attached to the side of it. Papa and Retta were seated in the two rocking chairs, but I couldn't make out their faces. Little Jack was standing near the screen door, and even from this distance I could see that his little stick body was rigid—and angry as a drenched cat.

Noah and I drew nearer, and I could hear my brother shouting at us. "Pidge! Tell Papa what you said!" he yelled, his voice cracking. "You said our mama was mentally ill! Now, ain't that what you said?"

I walked warily up the steps, stopping just short of my brother. His wiry limbs trembled with indignation—and a hint of something else. What was it? I took a step closer and he drew back, whimpering a little. His arms flew up in front of his face, and I knew what else I was seeing in Little Jack. It was fear. Fear that some of what he'd heard might be the truth.

"That *is* what I said, Little Jack," I admitted.

My brother turned to Papa and Aunt Retta. "See? She's lyin'! Papa, tell Pidge she's nothing but a big fat liar!"

Papa studied my brother, blinking with calm steady eyes. But I saw the edges of his jaw move, grinding against each other like two marbles in a sack. "She ain't lyin', Little Jack," my father said. "Your mama was very ill. Mentally ill. She was sick from sadness."

Little Jack's body went limp from head to toe, the anger just sort of seeping out of him. I think he'd known all along that I was right, but he just needed to hear Papa say it. I knelt down next to my brother, leaving Noah by the porch rail. My father went on.

"Remember Pippa, Little Jack? Remember how sad she was when her puppies died a few years back? Just howled and howled all day long. For weeks, it seemed like. Howling with a crazy kind of sadness that none of us could do a thing about. That's how your mama was. Just sick with sadness."

Little Jack walked over to Papa. His arms hung

down at his sides now, like a pair of broken twigs. "What was she so sad about?"

"Nobody knows. I don't think your mama even knew."

I listened to Papa's soft voice, very aware of Noah standing behind me. I was hesitant to sneak a sideways peek at him. What must he think of us Martins now, I wondered? If I were Noah Blore, I'd take off running this very minute and never look back.

My brother crawled into Papa's lap and curled up there, like one of Pippa's lost puppies. I glanced at Retta, whose rocking chair was creaking back and forth faster than a saw cutting through dogwood. When she finally slowed down to a reasonable speed, my aunt smiled over at me. Her eyes were moist.

Little Jack's eyes were open, but he looked about ready to pass out from exhaustion. His mouth twisted itself around like a pretzel, and then he asked, "If Mama was crazy, does that mean her soul went to hell?"

Aunt Retta's rocker picked up speed again. "Ain't no way your mama's soul went anywhere but heaven," she said emphatically. "For her, God reserved a spot in the very front pew."

I had to smile at that. Only Retta would see heaven as an interminable church service. To me, an eternity of listening to Reverend Tanner's sermons sounded a lot more like hell than heaven.

My aunt stopped rocking and leaned forward, until she was nearly nose to nose with Little Jack. "That woman was an angel," she said. "Just got called to heaven a little early is all."

Papa smoothed my brother's hair, letting his chin rest on Little Jack's head. "Why don't you get cleaned up for dinner?" he said.

Aunt Retta stood and held out a hand to my brother, who took it reluctantly. She led Little Jack across the porch, then turned to Noah. "You stayin' for dinner, Noah?" she asked.

Noah jumped, as if he'd been poked. Perhaps he thought we'd forgotten about him, standing there so soundlessly and listening to all of this. "Uhh . . . no, ma'am," he stammered. "I should probably be getting on home."

"Well, you're welcome to eat with us, if you change your mind." Retta and Little Jack went inside, but Noah made no move to leave the porch. He was eyeing Papa expectantly, and I realized he was hoping to find out what Doc Wheaton had been so intent on discussing this morning. Noah wasn't about to ask him, though. He was probably just waiting on me to do the asking for him.

"Papa?" I said. "What did Dr. Wheaton want with you at the train station?"

My father grunted wearily, rubbing his chest with one hand—the way I'd seen him do so many times. "Well, it seems that Doc Wheaton would like to offer me some money, Pidge."

Noah and I shot each other a look of surprise. "For what?" I asked angrily.

"To help me pay back our loan, I reckon."

I was confused, but Noah had it figured out immediately. "He doesn't think it's going to rain, does he?"

The corners of Papa's mouth twitched. "Sure looks that way."

"But what does—" I began.

"I borrowed money from the bank to pay for Miss Millie's trip out here," Papa explained. "To help out a few of the farmers who couldn't pay their share." Then Noah broke in, all agitated.

"And folks like my daddy and Denny's daddy are plannin' on paying you back, Mr. Martin, just like they done before. Soon as the oranges are ready for picking!" Noah sounded almost proud that his family had needed to borrow money from my father. But I guess he *was* proud, in a way. Proud to be associated with my papa. And too proud to accept charity from Dr. Wheaton, that was for sure.

"I know they are, Noah," my father said kindly. "But Dr. Wheaton is offering to pay the bank right now, before the oranges are even ripe." *If* they ever get ripe at all, I thought. And I knew Papa was thinking the same thing. If the crops didn't survive, people like Mr. Blore would have no way of repaying him—and he'd have to let the bank take our farm.

But I was still confused. "What does Dr. Wheaton get out of it, then?"

Papa laughed. "Well, I'll just have to pay *him* back, instead of paying the bank back."

"So he'll be buying us, too," I said dismally. First Mr. Giles's grocery store, now this. There didn't seem to be any way to get around that man and his money. Not in Frostfree anyway.

"Don't take it," Noah muttered, under his breath.

This wiped the smile clean off Papa's face. "What's that, son?"

Noah's jaws went tight, his temples tinged with pink. There was a stubborn streak in him that I'd never seen before. "Don't take his offer, sir." Then, realizing he probably shouldn't be giving orders to an adult, Noah added, "Please."

"And why shouldn't I?" my father asked him seriously.

A proud and positive Noah stared Papa straight in the eye. That boy had more faith in my father than the man had in himself. "'Cause it *is* going to rain, sir," he said.

# 14

IT RAINED THE FOLLOWING MORNING. As if by magic, we awoke to a sky draped in an endless purple gray, almost black.

I peered out my bedroom window, watching the shadowy clouds shift and move, like boulders. Papa and Aunt Retta were standing below me on the porch, their heads tilted back and up. Up, up, up, as if lowering their eyes might break the spell. I looked up, too. And, still in my pajamas, I ran downstairs to join them.

Knocking on Little Jack's door, I sped down the

hall, shouting, "*Rain!*" Then I raced noisily through the darkened parlor and onto the porch, all the while staring into the heavens, not daring to glance away. I didn't want to miss one moment of this miracle. I was too afraid it might disappear.

Suddenly, thunder crashed against the corners of the sky. Lightning filled the world with light, and I could see my aunt and my father leaning against the porch railing, watching the entire spectacle as if it were a show being put on especially for them. Papa's arm was wrapped around Retta's shoulder, his knuckles tight against his skin, and I squeezed in next to them. The rain crept, sticky and wet, through our clothing. Large, warm drops of water pummeled our foreheads and cheeks like pellets of hardened sand. We were soaked through and through, and we didn't even care.

The sky broke open again and again, emitting a greenish yellow light. And along with it came the rain, our precious rain, our hoped-for rain. The rain that would both rescue us and release us. It was as if all the water and thunder and lightning had been gathering up there for months, building on itself, gaining momentum, until finally . . . there had come a moment when the sky just had to let it go and spill over. That one last drop on a penny.

Another fork of lightning lit up our orange groves. The rows of trees shimmied in the wind, their wet leaves making a soft *swoosh* while they danced, as if whispering in gratitude. I was grateful, too.

More than that, I was in awe.

"Hey, y'all!" came a voice from above our heads.

We turned to see Little Jack, his body half hanging out the bedroom window. My brother's tongue protruded over his lower lip, poised and pointed upward in the hopes of catching a few enchanted drops of rain.

"You get back inside that window before you fall and break your head!" Aunt Retta shouted, but a new rumble of thunder overpowered her words, and I suspected that Little Jack wasn't listening to her anyway. Like us, he was too busy celebrating the rain's arrival, and I was relieved to hear the pure joy in my brother's laughter. Maybe the rain had released something in him as well, had helped to wash some of yesterday's anger away.

"We should *all* go back inside, before the lightning gets us," Papa advised.

"Do we have to?" I asked, not yet ready to leave the wildness and the wind. From behind four walls, the storm would soften into nothing but noise. And we would no longer be inside it, or a part of it.

"You heard your father," Aunt Retta said, but her voice was not stern. I could sense that she was as hesitant to leave the porch as I was. Rain streamed through her hair, framing her face in a silverish gray, and I saw that for once my aunt had not even thought to pull the strands back into a bun.

"How about some pecan waffles for breakfast?" she offered, and the three of us went inside to join Little Jack.

❊    ❊    ❊

By noon the phone was ringing like a church bell on Sunday. Folks from all over Frostfree were calling to congratulate my father, as if he were personally responsible for the downpour. Reverend Tanner wanted to host a jubilee at the church this evening, a "rain party" he called it. And my aunt was already busy organizing a potluck supper for the event.

We spent most of the afternoon baking and listening to Little Jack's running commentary on the fitful storm outside. Even the smells of warm corn-bread and sponge cake couldn't quite disguise the damp, moldy odor permeating the house, now that the rains had finally come. The cupboards and corners smelled like wet dishrags left out overnight, and I couldn't get enough of it.

"Lightning's headed way north now," Little Jack reported back to us, "but it's still raining like the devil."

"Watch your language, little man," Aunt Retta warned.

"Well, it is!" my brother retorted.

Retta sighed, wiping flour-coated fingers across

the front of her apron. "Why don't you do something useful, Little Jack, instead of using the Lord's name in vain?"

"I didn't say nothing about the Lord!" my brother exclaimed. "I was talking 'bout the devil!"

I busied myself with the cornbread, trying not to laugh. "Here's an idea, Little Jack," I said. "Why don't you write yourself a letter to Miss Millie, thanking her for bringing all this rain?"

My brother frowned. He couldn't write a whole lot better than he could read. "Will you help me with it?"

I glanced at Aunt Retta, who nodded appreciatively. Anything to get Little Jack out of the kitchen.

"You go on," she said, waving a hand toward the parlor.

I fished around for some paper and a pencil, then handed them to my brother. The two of us walked into the parlor, where we sat on the couch, staring out through the rain-streaked window.

"There," Little Jack said after a few minutes. "I'm done."

I read what he had written: *Dear Miss Millie: Thanks for bringing the rain. Sincerely, Little Jack Martin.*"

"That's it?" I said in disgust.

"I thanked her, didn't I?"

"Yes," I answered, "but you didn't tell her your true feelings. You need to let Miss Millie know how important the rain is to you—and to everybody here in Frostfree. Shoot, every last one of us could've lost our farms if it hadn't rained!"

Little Jack glared at the letter in my hand. "You're so busy *feeling* your feelings about the rain, you can finish the letter yourself!"

He bolted off the couch, like a stone freed from a slingshot. And I was left there holding Miss Millie's letter. Well, I thought. Maybe he was right. Maybe I should just finish the letter myself. Somebody had to let that woman know she'd brought a miracle to this town.

So I added a P.S. to Little Jack's message:

*P.S. Dear Miss Millie: It's Miriam. Remember me? I just thought you should know that rain has finally come to Frostfree, and we are mighty grateful. I guess you don't need to know all the particulars, but we might have lost our farm if the rains hadn't come pretty soon, seeing as how this was the longest drought we'd had in forty years. My father got the whole town together (well, almost the whole town) and they agreed to ask for your help. Papa even loaned money to some of the other growers because they were pretty close to losing their farms, too. So I'm writing to let you know that the rain arrived just in time. And it wouldn't have come at all, if not for you.*

*You saved us, Miss Millie. You delivered a miracle*

*right to our door, and we surely appreciate it. The
oranges do, too.*

> *Sincerely,*
> *Miriam (Pidge) Martin*

By the time I completed this additional note to
Miss Millie, my aunt had finished slicing her corn-
bread in the kitchen. I could hear her fussing at
Little Jack to get ready for the party, but I didn't feel
like getting up just yet.

I lingered on the couch, watching dark shadows
shift and dance across the floor. I could almost feel
the clouds heaving and rolling outside, bumping
against one another like impatient children,
building overhead—like a promise. A promise of
more water, and more rain. As much rain as we
wanted. As much as we needed. As much as we had
ever dared to ask for, maybe more.

"You 'bout ready, Pidge?" Aunt Retta asked
impatiently. My aunt had put on a rain hat and
slicker, and she shone like a bright-yellow flower
growing in our dim parlor.

"I'll be ready in a minute," I said, folding Miss
Millie's letter and placing it in an envelope. Then I
dashed upstairs to get ready for our rainy ride to the
church.

# 15

FIELDER STREET WAS A SLOUGH OF MUD, oozing straight through the middle of town. Some of the drivers ahead of us had already given up and parked on higher ground, walking the rest of the way to the Community Church in ankle-deep sludge.

Water beat down on our car like drumming fingers. The rain had now soaked through most people's lawns and flowerbeds, its overflow gathering in every available gutter and pothole. When Papa passed by the flooded sinkhole where the Giles's grocery store used to stand, he announced that we should rename it "Lake B & B."

"Or Lake Millie," I said, and everybody laughed.

We finally parked about a block away from the church and trekked the last few yards in the mud, each of us carrying a tray or a platter. As we neared the covered entryway in front of the meeting hall, a water-soaked figure hurriedly approached us, loaded down with containers of her own. It was Miss Jenny Barton, the church organist.

"Can you believe it?" she squealed. "The rain finally came, didn't it?"

"It surely did," Papa agreed, smiling crookedly at her from under his rain hat. I thought he looked sillier than a drenched scarecrow, and then it struck me who he reminded me of. My father was the spitting image of Denny Harper when he stood gazing at Dora with his "dopey" grin. I swallowed the sticky lump of anger at the base of my throat and turned away.

Little Jack was tugging at my arm, dragging me inside to enjoy the "rain party." But I suddenly felt deflated, washed out like the roads outside. What was wrong with me, anyway? Just minutes ago, I'd been so happy about the downpour.

"Hey, Pidge." It was Jean Hippleton, balancing an apple pie in both hands. "Where should I put this?"

My eyes swept the meeting hall. Aunt Retta and some of the ladies from the Auxiliary had set up tables of food near the back of the room.

"Over here," I said, leading the way for her.

Jean set the pie on the table, blowing on her hands. "Hot," she said, laughing softly.

"Hot pot," I said immediately, falling effortlessly into our old rhyming game from school.

She pointed to the table. "Hot pot spot." And we fell into helpless giggles.

When we'd recovered enough to control our laughter, Jean said, "Did you hear about Big Al?"

"Big Al? The alligator, you mean? The one that nearly ate your daddy's fishing pole?"

Jean giggled again. "Same one."

"What's he up to now? Nine or ten feet?"

Leaning forward, Jean whispered, "Well . . . turns out he's not a *he*. He's a *she!*"

"How do you know?"

"'Cause *she* just hatched a whole brood of baby gators! Right there on the shore of Sinkhole Lake! Papa saw them swimming around when he was fishing yesterday."

"Did they eat any more of his poles?" I asked, starting to laugh again.

But before she could answer me, Little Jack ran up to us, clean out of breath. "Guess who just pulled up to the church in his fancy car?" my brother wheezed.

I pivoted in time to see Dora Wheaton walking through the door. The bow in her hair was as big and wide as the smile on her face. And the chocolate cake her mother carried in could have fed half the town.

Mrs. Wheaton beamed at the entire crowd, as if this party were being thrown in her honor. Then she stepped aside as her husband entered behind her.

And—as I live and breathe—clutched in Dr. Wheaton's hand was a wad of money, nearly as big as his wife's chocolate cake!

"Where's Big Jack Martin?" the man boomed, as if he didn't know. Papa was standing right there in the middle of the room, although he *was* rather hidden from view. Surrounding him on all sides was a cluster of men, talking excitedly about the miraculous change in the weather.

"You lookin' for me, Win?" my father asked, his slow easy drawl coming out even slower than usual.

Doc Wheaton approached the group. "Yes, I am, Big Jack. And I have a proposition for you."

A few of the men appeared uneasy, most especially Denny Harper's father. But Papa seemed more amused than upset. "Go on," he said.

"Well," Dr. Wheaton began, "first of all let me state for the record that I am a man of science. I do not believe that the onset of this recent storm had a thing to do with your Rainmaker." He held up a hand before anyone could object. "But I am willing to concede that most of you do believe it. So . . . here's what I'm going to do. I will give one thousand dollars in cash—" up went the other hand, the one with the stack of money in it—"to anyone who will openly admit that Miss Millie Boze did *not* bring this rain."

The men exchanged glances. A thousand dollars was a lot of money, and they all wanted a piece of it.

"But she did," Papa replied. "It rained within forty-eight hours of Miss Millie's arrival, and that's good enough for me."

Some of the men cheered. A few of the onlookers shouted in agreement. I noticed Noah and Denny yelling along with them, from the other side of the meeting hall. I quickly hid behind Jean, unsure of Noah's feelings for me now that he had learned about Mama and her "illness."

Dr. Wheaton smiled thinly at my father. "Scientific proof, Big Jack. That's all I need. Either that, or admit you are wrong. Then this money is yours."

"With interest?" Papa said, grinning. And the room erupted in laughter. Even Doc Wheaton chuckled before slapping the pile of money with his free hand.

"I'm as grateful for this rain as the rest of you," he said earnestly. "That's why I'm here celebratin' tonight. But I'd just like somebody here to allow the possibility that Miss Millie had nothing to do with it!"

Dr. Wheaton's desperate gaze took in the entire congregation. I think he wanted to believe in the Rainmaker as much as any of us did. He was just too stubborn to abandon all those precious principles of his.

"I ain't admittin' any such thing," my father said softly, "but I do appreciate the offer."

Doc Wheaton stood uncertainly in the center of the huge room. He examined the money in his hand and shrugged, then wadded up the bills and jammed them into his pocket.

His wife swept past him, still carrying her ten-gallon pastry. "Who wants cake?" she said brightly. Then Mrs. Wheaton swathed a path through the crowd, setting her enormous dessert on the table, right next to Jean and me.

Jean scooted over, her eyes big as saucers. I was rooted to the floor—a fence post struck dumb. I watched Dora's mother coolly cut her cake into thirty-two symmetrical slivers, as if her husband was in the habit of offering a thousand dollars to a room full of people every day.

Perhaps he was.

"Pidge, honey," she said sweetly, "could you help me serve?"

"Yes'm," I replied.

I handed a plate and fork to Jean, who took them wordlessly and went off to sit with Martha Jarvis.

People had begun to mill about the hall again, some of them even approaching the table as I offered up slices of Mrs. Wheaton's cake.

Dora and Denny were secluded in a corner, holding hands and whispering. Across the room I observed Miss Jenny talking with a group of women from the church. She was laughing, shaking her head like a wet dog, and I thought—just for a moment—that she seemed almost pretty. Then I saw Papa staring over at her, too, and smiling.

"Well, what d'you think?" said a voice from behind me.

It was Noah Blore, with Little Jack nipping at his heels like an adoring pet. At first I thought Noah was talking about my father and Miss Jenny. But then I realized he must be referring to Dr. Wheaton's incredible offer.

"I think Doc Wheaton's money is safe," I answered. "No one's going to tell him Miss Millie is a fake. But I don't think anybody here can prove she *isn't*."

Little Jack stomped his tiny foot on the wood floor. "Papa can," he said confidently. "Papa's gonna win that thousand dollars. You just wait and see."

My eyes met Noah's and I detected some amusement there, before self-consciously looking away.

"Well . . . I guess that's what we're gonna have to do, Little Jack," Noah agreed.

# 16

*Frostfree Observer*
**Wednesday, July 26, 1939**

## RAINMAKER CHARMS THE SKIES!

Heavy rains and showers, which growers
hailed with delight, poured down on
Frostfree, Florida, yesterday and last
night, ending a drought clearly destined
for the record books! After nearly
five months without a drop of rain,
farmers in this small orange-growing
community sent for "Rainmaker"
Millie Boze from Oxford, Mississippi,
and she performed the impossible.
Miss Boze brought rain to the orange
groves of this small town, delivering a
miracle to every citrus grower in the area.

"Well, this should be all the proof Doc Wheaton needs," Aunt Retta sniffed during breakfast the following morning. "Says right here in the newspaper that Miss Millie brought rain to our orange groves."

Papa laughed, helping himself to a large spoonful of scrambled eggs. "If you believe everything you read in the *Frostfree Observer*," he said, "the Depression is over, and the South won the War Between the States."

I was standing behind Retta, reading over her shoulder. "There's a quote from Dr. Wheaton later on in the article," I told him. "It says: 'This is nothing more than the support of witchcraft against science.'"

"And that's in the newspaper, too, Retta," Papa said, grinning at her.

My aunt patted her hair indignantly and stood up from the table. "Well, do you want the man's money or don't you?" she huffed.

"I could surely use it," Papa admitted. "But I can't prove Miss Millie brought the rain to Frostfree. And I'm sure not going to tell all the farmers in this town that they wasted their money on a crook."

I thought Papa was being just as stubborn as Doc Wheaton, but I didn't say so. After all, I could be pretty stubborn myself.

"Who needs his old money anyway?" I said, piling eggs onto my plate.

Papa and Aunt Retta gaped at me, like I'd lost my mind.

"Well?" I went on. "It's raining now, ain't it? So the oranges will be all right, and we can keep the farm."

Papa looked uncomfortable. "It's not so easy, Pidge," he said. "With a good crop, most everybody can pay me back. And that will cover the loan, I reckon, but not much else."

I glanced out the window. Rain still poured from a slate gray sky. It shimmered on the branches of the orange trees, like strands of silver. Not much else, I thought? What else was there but the oranges?

"House needs a new roof," Retta said matter-of-factly, "and your daddy could use a new tractor, too."

"Not to mention clothes and shoes for you and Little Jack," Papa added, with a hint of a smile.

"I could get a job," I said, knowing at once how ridiculous this sounded. During these hard times, men were lined up at the courthouse every week seeking employment. Who would ever hire me?

"We'll be fine, darlin'," my father assured me. "Just don't go looking Dr. Wheaton's gift in the mouth."

What gift, I wondered? Dora's father hadn't given us anything, as far as I could tell.

Little Jack charged into the kitchen, one strap of

his overalls still unhooked. "What's for breakfast?" he shouted, plopping himself down next to me.

"Nothin', unless you wash your hands first," Aunt Retta replied, and he got up again. I watched my aunt scrubbing at his hands with a damp rag, and I thought about that money of Dr. Wheaton's. There just had to be a way to get at it without giving in to him, I thought. The trick was finding out how.

Papa stood, wiping his chin with a napkin. "By the way, Retta," he said, a little too casually, "I invited company for supper this evening. So you might want to set another place at the table."

My aunt stopped rubbing at Little Jack's dirty fingers. "Oh, Jack," she said, smiling at him. "I'm so pleased. What time should we be expecting her?"

"'Bout six or so," he answered. "Thought you could make those tasty spareribs of yours and maybe some black-eyed peas."

Little Jack stared at Papa, his mouth open. "Black-eyed peas!" he exclaimed, making a face. "Who'd wanna come all the way over here to eat *those?*"

Aunt Retta winked at my brother, then gave him a gentle shove toward the table. "Miss Jenny Barton, that's who," she said, beaming.

Little Jack sat down next to me, scowling. "What's that old Miss Jenny Barton doing, comin' to our house for supper?" he said to me under his breath.

I scowled back at him, not answering. I knew

exactly what she was doing. And I hoped her car got stuck in a ditch on the way over here.

❋   ❋   ❋

Miss Jenny's car did not get stuck. It pulled into our muddy drive at six o'clock on the dot, and she climbed out of the front seat, looking more dressed up than was fitting for a simple supper at the Martin house.

"Hey, Retta," she said, handing my aunt a plate of lemon-and-spice cookies. "Thought I'd bring a little something for dessert."

My aunt patted her hair so hard, I thought it must be falling out of her head. Then she led Miss Jenny into the kitchen.

"Evenin', Pidge," Miss Jenny said to me, as she passed by the parlor. I was sitting on the couch reading a book and pretending not to hear her. I didn't acknowledge the woman, but I raised my eyes enough to see her white shoes, now caked with mud, tapping their way into our kitchen.

Papa came down a few minutes later, wearing his Sunday shirt and shoes. Shoot, you would have thought the mayor was coming for supper, the way folks were carrying on tonight.

I sat silently at the table while we ate, listening to Aunt Retta trying to make polite conversation with Miss Jenny.

"Where was it you said you lived before coming to Frostfree?" my aunt asked, passing the peas my way.

"Tampa," Miss Jenny replied. "My husband worked at the boat docks there."

*Husband!* Miss Jenny had been married? I shot a quick glance at my father, who seemed maddeningly unsurprised by this piece of news.

Miss Jenny went on. "After he . . . well, after he was gone, I decided to get out of the big city and move to someplace a bit more quiet."

"Where'd he *go?*" Little Jack asked. Wouldn't you know? I wanted to crawl right under the table and stay there. That child didn't have the sense of a tree stump.

But Miss Jenny gave my brother a tiny smile, as if he amused her. "He died, Little Jack."

"Died? Well, how'd he—*ouch!*"

I gave him a swift kick under the table, and he turned to glare at me. This time Miss Jenny actually laughed out loud.

"My husband worked at the loading docks down at the harbor," she explained to him. "One day, as I was preparing his supper, there was this huge explosion. The house shook and rattled like it had been hit by a hurricane. And even though the docks were miles away, somehow I just knew . . ." she fiddled with the napkin on her knees, then leveled her gaze on my brother. "Even before the phone rang, I knew that the ship he was on had exploded. A premonition, I guess. And I was right. They told me it was a gasoline leak, or some such thing. No one survived the blast."

We sat, suspended, after hearing her story. Even Little Jack was silent. The only sound was the steady beating of the rain overhead, like an army relentlessly marching across our roof.

I focused on my lap, wishing I didn't know this new fact about Miss Jenny. It changed things. Finally, I dared to lift my head and take a peek at her. She was sitting up against the back of the chair, her shoulders straight and her lips firm. But everything else about her was perfectly calm—the way she sometimes looked when she played the organ at the Community Church on Sundays.

As I stared at Miss Jenny across from me, it suddenly seemed that a different person was sitting at our table, a woman I had never seen before. A woman I had never tried to see. And a sick feeling crept into my stomach and up into my throat. I felt the same way I'd felt that day my father had carried in a dollhouse for my birthday, instead of the rocking horse I'd been expecting.

I had been so sure . . . and I had been so wrong.

Little Jack was the first to recover from Miss Jenny's incredible tale. "My mama died, too," he said, as if trying to top her story. But then I realized he was just trying to connect Miss Jenny's tragedy to something he already knew about. In his own tactless little way, my brother was offering his friendship to this woman. But I still sat motionless in my chair, mute as one of Mrs. Wheaton's statues.

"I know about your mama, Little Jack," Miss Jenny said. "That must have been very difficult for you."

"Oh, it was," he answered seriously, and I almost kicked him again. What did he know about it? Little Jack had been only a baby at the time.

"She left me a real pretty bracelet, though," my brother went on. "Wanna see it?"

Miss Jenny cocked her head toward me, and I met her gaze. Still watching me, she addressed Little Jack. "I don't know about that, honey," she said quietly. "Seems kind of a private thing, just between the two of you. Don't you think?"

Little Jack smacked the tabletop with his tiny fist. "Naaah. My mama wouldn't mind. Would she, Pidge?"

I was instantly aware of everyone's eyes upon me, most especially Aunt Retta's. I knew what they wanted me to do. But I couldn't. I just couldn't give that much of my mama away.

"Maybe now is not such a good time," I said, folding my napkin and placing it on the table next to my plate. "May I be excused?"

"Well, I don't—" began Retta.

"Course you can, darlin'," Papa said. His dark eyes regarded me kindly, but for some reason this made me feel small and spiteful. Like my father was just being sorry for me, instead of trying to understand how I really felt. Like maybe he thought there was something wrong with me for not wanting to share my mama's jewelry with any old person who came over for supper.

As I stood up to leave, I couldn't help noticing Aunt Retta's exaggerated shake of the head. No one said a word to me. That's probably because they were going to start talking about me as soon as I exited the room.

"Pidge?" It was Miss Jenny. "If you get to feeling better, I brought some cookies for dessert."

I stood uncomfortably in the doorway, wondering if there were some way I could sit back down again without surrendering my pride—along with Mama's bracelet.

"Thanks," I mumbled. Then I fled upstairs before any tears could begin.

# 17

I DIDN'T COME BACK DOWN until after Little Jack was asleep. The rain had finally abated for a while, and from outside my window earlier I'd heard him laughing with Papa and Miss Jenny on the porch. Then the screen door slammed and Aunt Retta came out to announce that the dishes were done, and it was time for all good little boys to be in bed. This was followed by my brother's usual string of arguments, excuses, promises, and pleadings. But eventually, my aunt got him into his pajamas and safely tucked in for the night.

My stomach was growling by that time, since I'd

barely touched my dinner, and I knew I couldn't stay up here in my room forever. I'd never last until breakfast. Peering out my window, I saw Papa and Miss Jenny walk down the porch steps and across our small lawn into the orange groves. They quickly disappeared into the dark rows of trees, and I had a sudden memory of my father taking me on that very same walk, just a year or so ago.

"All this will belong to you, Pidge," he'd said to me. Was he saying those words now? Again? To somebody else?

The light from the porch below flickered, and I wondered if some distant lightning might be crackling over someone else's farm, over someone else's orange groves. Aunt Retta sat quietly beneath the lamp, rocking in her favorite spot—just in front of the large parlor window. And I couldn't help thinking. What would happen to her if Miss Jenny's visits became more frequent, and more permanent?

I quickly made my way downstairs and onto the porch. The wet boards creaked under the weight of me, and my aunt smiled. Her eyes were closed, but she spoke to me as she rocked.

"All cried out, are you?"

I sat in the other rocker, staring out at the blackened shadows of the orange trees. "Yes'm."

She chuckled softly and opened her eyes. "Life's a chancy thing, ain't it?"

I nodded, not exactly sure what she meant. But I thought she was talking about taking chances on people. If you counted on people, they could let you down. If you loved people, they could die.

I sucked in a breath, letting it out real slow. "Am I terrible?" I said finally.

Aunt Retta stopped rocking, staring at me. "Why would you ask me a thing like that, Pidge?"

"Because I like her," I said, almost defiantly. "I like Miss Jenny."

"Well, that's not so terrible," she said with a laugh. "I like her, too."

My aunt didn't understand. She hadn't lost her mama when she was only seven years old. And she'd never had to watch her own daddy courting somebody else at the dinner table. "But I *can't* like her. Don't you see?"

I could tell that Aunt Retta was attempting to see, for my sake. But she was having a hard time of it. I tried again.

"Well, what if Miss Jenny and Papa get . . . ummm . . . you know, married?"

Retta resumed her rocking. "So what if they do?"

"What will happen to you then?" I cried. "Where will you go?"

My aunt looked shocked. "I ain't goin' nowhere!" she said. "This is my house, too, and I live here."

The notion of my aunt coexisting with Miss

Jenny under one roof seemed mighty unlikely to me. Somehow, I couldn't see her fighting with Miss Jenny over who would sweep the parlor or who would prepare the pot roast. Like Retta always said, *too many cooks spoiled the broth.* And I knew my aunt would never surrender her kitchen duties to anyone else.

"Aren't you afraid she'll take your place?" I cried.

Aunt Retta stared at me for a long moment. "Ain't *my* place you're worried about, is it?"

I couldn't answer that. My throat tightened. And without meaning to, I started to cry again. My aunt pushed herself up from her rocking chair and came around to stand beside me. She stroked my hair awkwardly, like someone petting a strange animal. But then, I was strange. Everyone knew it. Noah had even come right out and said so.

"Nobody wants to steal the memory of your mama, Pidge. It's not there for the stealing anyway. It doesn't *belong* to anybody, least of all you. So you might as well just let it go."

But that was the one thing I couldn't do. Aside from the box of trinkets upstairs, memories were the only thing I had left of my mother. I had to save them for Little Jack. And if those memories didn't belong to *me*, then who? Who would take care of them if I didn't? Who would make sure the memories never got lost? Or forgotten? Certainly not Papa, I thought angrily. The way he was mooning over Miss Jenny tonight said it all. He was starting to forget about Mama already. And Retta hadn't even lived here with my mother, so how much could she really remember?

"You hold on so tight to things, honey," my aunt said softly. "To memories, and people . . . and the way you think things ought to be . . . "

I sat up then, glaring at her. "What do you mean the *way things ought to be?*"

Retta's hand went to her hair, then stopped. "You always want things to be a certain way, Pidge. Your way. And when they aren't, you get angry. And then you let it build and build inside you, until all that anger just comes pourin' out of you." She peered up at the dark wall of clouds above our heads. "Just like them rain clouds," she said. "When they finally let go, it's quite a storm, ain't it?"

My aunt smiled at me then. But I didn't smile back. "You don't know every little thing about me," I said. And she didn't disagree. But she didn't stop talking, either.

"All I'm saying is . . . let people be wrong sometimes. Let yourself be wrong sometimes. The world won't come to an end."

I rocked for a while, not saying anything. In the distance, I heard the low rumble of thunder and then I saw a pinpoint of light making its way toward us. Papa must have been showing Miss Jenny around the orange groves with his flashlight, I thought. Shoot. How many oranges could they possibly see at night with that thing?

Then it struck me that they probably weren't out there looking at oranges.

"Yoo hoo!" Aunt Retta shouted to them. "See who came out to join us?"

Papa and Miss Jenny entered the halo of light from the porch lamp, and I saw my father quickly drop her hand.

"Feeling better?" he asked me.

"Yes, sir," I answered, and Jenny Barton smiled brightly.

"How about some of those cookies now?" she offered, scurrying past me and my aunt to fetch her plate from the kitchen. Papa watched her go, squinting against the brightness of the light above her head, and the screen door slammed shut behind her. He leaned his face back and up, taking in the starless sky above our heads.

"It's gonna come down again," he said.

"Any minute now," Aunt Retta agreed.

I didn't get up from the rocking chair. "Felt good to get a little break, though," I replied.

Then Miss Jenny came out onto the porch with her cookies.

After Jenny left, Aunt Retta took herself off to
bed, and I helped my father straighten up in the
kitchen. We worked together in comfortable silence,
and I thought about the hundreds of nights we'd
spent just like this, putting the dishes away and
wiping down the table and counters. For the first
time in my life, I considered the very real possibility
that these nights together might come to an end.
That feeling overwhelmed me again, the same one
I'd had during dinner. The sense that everything I
was seeing had suddenly changed, and I was no
longer looking at the same room. My stomach
fluttered, and I had to sit down.

"Pidge?" Papa asked. "You all right?" There it
was. That question again. But I'd given up denying
it by this time.

"No," I answered dully.

My father sat down across from me at the table.
"Is this about Jenny?"

"Partly," I said, knowing that I couldn't blame
everything on her, as much as I'd wanted to earlier.
My eyes swept the room, taking in everything that
was familiar about this kitchen. The scratches in the
table, the baseboards in need of paint, the leaky
faucet my father had fixed only a couple of months
ago. This room wasn't big and it wasn't fancy, but
until tonight I'd always known my place in it.

"What's going to happen to us?" I asked.

Papa scratched his chin. "I guess everybody wonders about that, most of the time."

"No. I mean, what's going to happen to our family?" I pressed. Then I just couldn't help myself. "Are you gonna marry Miss Jenny?" I blurted out.

My father threw his head back and laughed out loud. "Lordy, I don't know, Pidge," he said, slapping one knee with his hand. Then Papa saw me frowning, and he tried to be more serious. "Would it be so awful, darlin'?"

"It would be . . . different," I said, after a thoughtful pause.

"And you don't want that." It wasn't a question. I nodded hesitantly, and Papa sighed. "Sometimes things change, Pidge. No, not sometimes. *All* the time. And that's the way it should be. People change. They grow up. They go away. Some of them even die."

I sulked, studying my hands in my lap and thinking about Papa and my mama—and then Miss Jenny.

"I ain't planning on forgetting your mother, if that's what you're fuming about." My neck snapped back up in surprise. That was exactly what I was fuming about, but I wondered how he knew.

"Your mama was the love of my life, Pidge. Always will be. But she wouldn't want me hanging on to her forever, now would she?"

I didn't see why not.

Papa rubbed a hand across his chest and then through his hair. "Let me tell you a little story about you and your mama," he said.

I leaned forward eagerly. My father rarely told stories, and I couldn't remember him ever once revealing anything personal about my mother.

"Back when you were about five or six, your mama would walk you to school every day. I remember watching the two of you leave the house each morning, holding hands and turning left at the end of the drive. Then she'd walk back to school and fetch you. Every afternoon. And there you'd be, the pair of you. Still holding hands, until you finally stepped up onto the porch. Do you remember that?"

I shook my head sadly. I didn't remember it at all.

"Well," he went on, "one day the two of you came back—same as always. But you were running on ahead of her. Just tearing down the drive, like a dog after a rabbit. You rushed inside the house and told me all about your day at school, then went straight upstairs to play with your dolls."

I made a face, not wanting to be reminded that I used to play with dolls. I waited for Papa to go on with his story, but he didn't. "That's it?" I said, disappointed.

"Yep. That's it. You just ran upstairs, like you didn't even care."

I had clearly missed something here. "Didn't care about what?"

"That your mama had let go of your hand."

I tried to picture myself, that little girl running toward the house and her dolls. But I couldn't see her, any more than I could imagine the woman following her down the gravelly drive, the distance between mother and daughter lengthening like twine from a spool. I desperately hoped that my mama had not been angered or hurt by that little girl.

"A year later, Little Jack was born," Papa added, and this calmed me. Perhaps I hadn't really done any permanent damage to my mother, I thought, when I'd run away from her like that. After all, it was probably a lot easier for my mama to take care of Little Jack when she didn't have to walk *me* to school every day.

Then I thought I saw what my father was really trying to say. My mama hadn't been the only one to let go. I was the one who was ready to run on ahead, all by myself. What I'd done had probably wounded my mother's feelings a bit, but children everywhere did it all the time. People grew up. People let go.

"So you're saying Little Jack wouldn't be here if it wasn't for me?" I asked. This did not sit well, knowing that I might be responsible for something so important, so . . . permanent.

But Papa smiled, and I knew he was remembering something I couldn't see. "Well . . . we were thinking about having another baby anyway," he admitted, "but seeing you get so independent all of a sudden *did* help us decide."

I thought again about that little girl running down the drive, and I realized that my mother had probably been more relieved than hurt as she watched me scamper away. This thought was not comforting, but it did make me feel a little less guilty. Then I wondered how my father would have reacted, had he been in her place, seeing me sprint off toward the house all by myself. And I knew the answer to that one without even stopping to think about it. Papa would have been proud.

"Well," I said, scooting my chair back and standing up. "If you *do* decide to marry Miss Jenny, just don't let her mess with Aunt Retta's kitchen."

Papa nodded. "I'll try and remember that piece of advice," he said solemnly.

But—as I live and breathe—I couldn't figure out why he was smiling.

# 18

R~AIN.~

Rain, rain, rain. The next day brought us plenty more, along with sharp gusts of wind that kept slamming the screen door shut. But it also brought us some unexpected correspondence.

"Look at this!" Little Jack shouted. He came bounding into my room, waving something white and rectangular over his head. He slapped it down on my desk, next to Mama's box of jewelry and knickknacks.

"What is it?"

"A letter! And I think it's for us."

I snatched the letter from my desktop, trying to make out the spidery script scrawled across the front of the envelope. The handwriting was jerky and thin, as if someone had taken a knife and scratched the address onto the paper.

"What's it say?" Little Jack demanded.

"Hold your horses," I said irritably. "I'm trying to read. It says: *To Miss Miriam and Master Jack Martin.*"

"Master Jack! Who's he?"

"That's you," I said.

My brother wrinkled his nose. "I ain't no master!"

"It's a form of Mister," I said. "I think it means you're not married—or something like that."

Little Jack shook his head, as if there were just too many things in this world that would never make sense to him. I hurriedly opened the letter, scanning its contents.

"It's from Millie Boze!" I exclaimed. "She wrote back to us."

I sat down on the edge of my bed, and Little Jack scooted in next to me as I read the letter aloud to him:

*Dear Miriam and Little Jack,*

*Thank you so much for your lovely letter. It's nice to know that rain finally came to Frostfree, although I* am hardly surprised. Rain seems to follow me around like a hungry dog, and I truly don't know why. Nor do I know precisely how my rain vigils operate. But I do know one thing, and this is for you in particular, Miriam. I know for a fact that I did not deliver a miracle to your town.

I am not a miracle worker, dear. The rain that you are now enjoying would have come to Frostfree sooner or later. I just helped it along a little. I like to think that I coaxed those raindrops out of the sky with my own special brand of magic.

You say this was the longest drought your town has had in forty years? Well, then. The rain was probably just building itself up all this time, waiting for someone like me to come along and set it free. But I haven't quite figured out how that part of the magic works yet.

If anyone delivered a miracle, it was all of you. Your father and all of the other farmers, right there in Frostfree. They believed in something enough to work together for it, and to make a few sacrifices along the way. So don't you go thinking I'm more than I really am. I'm just plain old Millie Boze from Oxford, Mississippi. But I'm always glad to be of service. You take care, and give my regards to your father.

Sincerely,
Miss Millie

I set the letter in my lap, not quite certain how to decipher its contents. Had Miss Millie brought the rain or not? And if she hadn't, did that mean Dr. Wheaton was right after all? Was Millie Boze a fake?

Little Jack sat up on his knees beside me, waving both hands in the air like he was about to take off in flight.

"This is Papa's proof!" he said excitedly.

I regarded him skeptically. "Proof of what?"

"Proof that Miss Millie didn't bring the rain! She says so herself in that letter. Now all Papa has to do is show it to Doc Wheaton and tell him that she had nothing to do with it. Then he gets the thousand dollars."

"Miss Millie didn't say she had nothing to do with it, Little Jack. She just said she didn't deliver a miracle."

"What's the difference?"

I didn't know for certain, but I was pretty sure there was one. And anyway, I didn't think Dr. Wheaton would part with his money, just because of a handwritten denial from Miss Millie.

Little Jack grabbed impatiently for the letter on my lap. "If you ain't gonna do nothing about it, then I will," he said, jumping off the bed and heading for the door.

I didn't have a good feeling about this. My brother's impulses generally got him into trouble.

"What are you going to do?"

"Gonna take this letter over to Dora, that's what. See if she'll show it to her daddy!"

"No!" I yelped, diving off the bed to grab him, but he took off quick as a squirrel up a tree. My brother was down the steps and out the front door before I could do little more than call out his name. And I knew he'd do exactly what he said he would do. Little Jack would show that letter to Dora and . . . and then what? Would she laugh in his face? Refuse to help him?

I didn't think so. As much as I disliked Dora Wheaton, I believed she had always been on Miss Millie's side. She'd been out there at the train station on the day the Rainmaker arrived, and—as I remember it—Dora was hooting and hollering along with all the rest of us.

Then again . . . I didn't think Dora had it in her to defy her own father, even if her defiance meant something as simple as showing him a letter. I'd seen Dr. Wheaton when he was angry, and if I were Dora, I wouldn't have crossed him, either. Well, maybe for Little Jack I might. He was my brother after all. And Dora liked him, too, I knew that. Better than she liked me, when it came right down to it.

She'd taken a shine to my brother and the feeling was—to my surprise—mutual. So maybe Dora would at least show the letter to her father. For Little

Jack's sake. But it probably wouldn't do any good, and my brother would just end up being disappointed and hurt.

Well, whatever Dora did, I couldn't do a thing about it. And I couldn't do a thing to stop Little Jack, either. If I ran after him, he would just run faster. I couldn't protect him from every little thing in the world, now could I? Hadn't Aunt Retta told me so, just last night? I was going to have to let him make his own mistakes from now on.

But my aunt hadn't told me how hard that was going to be.

I ran to the window and watched Little Jack tearing off down the road toward town. His skinny stick legs kicked out behind him like a knock-kneed colt's. And I kept on watching him, long after he made a sudden turn into the woods and vanished from sight, disappearing under the lush overhang of the cypress trees.

❊  ❊  ❊

Dr. Wheaton's sleek silver Packard pulled into our drive a little before sundown. Little Jack jumped out of the backseat, heading up the porch steps like his pants were on fire.

"Papa!" he shouted, the screen door banging loudly behind him. "Doc Wheaton's here! And he's got something to show you!"

176

I peeked down from the top of the stairs and saw Dora and Dr. Wheaton standing awkwardly on the landing, just inside the front door. Their shoes were covered in mud, and Doc Wheaton's big black umbrella dripped water onto the hardwood floor. I heard a noise from below and saw Papa and Aunt Retta following Little Jack out of the kitchen, my aunt hurriedly wiping flour across the front of her apron.

"Evenin', Win," Papa said, calm as you please. "Won't you come in?"

The man was already in, but I guess my father wanted to make it official. Leastways, he wanted Doc Wheaton to know that invitations were generally required before stepping into someone else's home.

The two of them took a seat in the parlor, leaving Dora and Aunt Retta standing uncomfortably in the doorway. Little Jack ran upstairs to join me on the top step, where I sat, shamelessly eavesdropping as usual. Dora's eyes followed him up the stairs, and, noticing me for the first time, she fluttered a tiny finger wave at me. I nodded, unable to move. From up here, it appeared that her father was not very pleased to be out this evening, nor did he seem particularly friendly.

"Got a letter in the mail yesterday," he said, pulling a long slip of paper from his coat pocket.

*Yesterday?* But Miss Millie's letter had arrived only this afternoon.

Dora's father began reading the letter aloud, but Papa interrupted. "No use quotin' it, Win," he said quietly. "Got the same letter myself."

*What?* Little Jack and I exchanged a quick glance. Why would Millie Boze be writing letters to Papa and Dr. Wheaton, I wondered? Or had they written to her first? None of this made a lick of sense.

Aunt Retta had given up all pretense of listening in on the men's conversation. She entered the parlor and plopped herself down on the sofa, her soiled apron still tied about her waist. Dora sat on the bottom step, signaling for me and Little Jack to come down and join her. I was reluctant to take part in any conspiracies involving Dora Wheaton, but my brother was at her side before I could even grab ahold of him. Besides, I was tired of listening without being able to see what was going on. At least the lower staircase allowed a better view of the parlor. So I scooted down to within three steps of Dora and Little Jack, continuing to listen.

"You wrote for information from the U.S. Department of Meteorology?" Dr. Wheaton's tone was incredulous.

Little Jack turned his head toward me, obviously confused. I shrugged back down at him. I wasn't sure what that word meant, either, but I thought meteorology had something to do with the weather.

"I do write letters from time to time," Papa said, and I could hear the laughter in his voice.

Doc Wheaton seemed to ignore that remark. "Well, if you got the same letter, then you know as well as I do that your Rainmaker had nothing to do with this storm." He smacked the paper with the back of one hand, as if this gave the letter's contents more validity. "A tropical depression started in the Gulf a week before her arrival, and it was already headed this way."

"I reckon that's true," Papa said. "Ain't denying it."

Dora's father stared at him, as if he had just been introduced to the fool of the world.

"But you're still saying that Miss Millie brought the rain here *with* her? From the Gulf of Mexico?"

"Ain't saying that, either."

Doc Wheaton delivered that smile of his that wasn't really a smile at all. He was waiting for Papa to let the other shoe fall.

My father waved the sheet of paper in his hand. "This letter is mighty good at presenting the facts," he said finally, "but sometimes a situation calls for more than that. What I got here is a bunch of scientists from Washington who believe in numbers and weather patterns. But what I got *here*—" Papa dropped the letter and pointed through our rain-spattered window, indicating what lay beyond the window and the porch and even the orange trees, "is a bunch of people who believe they did something constructive by summoning a little old lady here from Mississippi. And I won't ever let them think otherwise. Not even for a thousand dollars."

Dora's father studied the letter lying on the floor. He didn't look up for a long time. "We're all in this together, Jack," he said finally, still not raising his eyes. "I'm offering you the money. I want you to have it. I want *everyone* to have it, if they need it."

"Course they need it," Papa said, getting as close to being angry as I'd ever seen him, "but they don't want it. Not on your terms."

I stole a peek at Dora, wondering how she was taking all of this. But I couldn't see her face. Little Jack whispered something to her and she whispered something in response, with all the unruffled patience I seemed to lack, especially where my brother was concerned. This show of intimacy angered me, and yet I was grateful that Little Jack had found a friend. Even if this particular friend was a girl who could never truly be a friend to *me*. Dora had said and done too many things I wasn't likely to forget. The girl bore an irksome resemblance to Denny Harper in that regard. But, like Noah had said, Dora was here. Whether I liked it or not.

Dr. Wheaton's voice interrupted my thoughts. "And what terms are those, Jack?"

"That their faith—and their money—were wasted on a dream."

Dora's father planted both elbows on his knees, rubbing his hands together. "What can I do, then?" he asked.

My father tipped back in his chair, resting his head in the palms of his hands. "I've been thinking about that . . ." he replied, a smile escaping from the corners of his mouth.

"I'll bet you have," Dr. Wheaton said, and they chuckled quietly together, although I couldn't see what was so funny.

Papa leaned forward then, and I could tell that he was excited. "What if we were to set up a cooperative, almost like a food bank? Folks put money in when they can, and folks take it out when they really need it. But only if everyone in the group agrees. Sort of like a group insurance policy."

Dr. Wheaton scratched his chin. "And you would start it with my thousand dollars?" He was frowning, but I could see that he was seriously considering the idea.

Papa grinned at him. "Thanks for offerin', Win." He stuck out his hand, and Dr. Wheaton regarded it warily, as if it were a venomous animal waiting to strike. When he finally shook it, I wasn't sure what had just happened. But it must have been good, because Aunt Retta immediately stood up and untied her apron.

"How about some dessert, Dr. Wheaton?" she said brightly. "We have a chocolate cake in the kitchen." Then she poked her head out and around the parlor door. "Children with big ears are welcome to join us, too," she added.

# 19

DURING THE NIGHT, there was a blessed break in the weather. Streaks of late morning sunlight brushed my eyes awake, as bird song ricocheted through the orange trees outside. I hurriedly opened my bedroom window, breathing in the cool air that always seemed to follow the rain, and I listened as footsteps tapped across the porch below, followed by a soft knock on the front door.

"Pidge?" Aunt Retta called up the stairs. "You got company!"

Company? Who could be here to see me at this hour? I glanced at the clock beside my bed and was surprised to see that it was nearly noon. Shoot. I hadn't even brushed my teeth yet. Maybe I could just tell whomever it was to come back later.

Little Jack threw open the door to my room, bouncing across the floor and onto the bed. "Your boyfriend's here," he said smugly.

"What?" I said, my tongue still thick with sleep.

"Noah Blo-o-o-ore," he sang, and I wanted to wipe that smirk clean off his face.

Instead, I panicked. My hair was a mass of tangles, my eyelids puffy from oversleep, and I was still in my pajamas!

"I can't go down there," I said to Little Jack. "I look awful!"

"Tell me somethin' I don't already know," he said, grinning at me.

I threw my pillow at him, but he ducked. "Could you ask him to wait until I can get cleaned up?" I begged.

My brother scrutinized me, up and down. "How long's that gonna be?"

"I don't know. Half hour or so. Why don't you show him around the farm or something?"

Little Jack's eyes darted to the box on top of my desk. "Can I show him some of Mama's jewelry?"

I sincerely doubted that Noah would care about

a box of brooches and bracelets, but he would probably be too polite to say so. "Fine," I said.

My brother grabbed the box and tucked it under his arm, as if it were a live thing trying to escape. He tore out of my room and down the stairs, shouting, "Noah! Look what I got here!"

I descended twenty minutes later, my face scrubbed and my hair and teeth brushed. I'd even run a bit of Aunt Retta's lipstick across my mouth and dabbed something pink and powdery over both cheeks.

As I entered the kitchen, everyone gathered around the table stared up at me. My cheeks went three shades pinker.

"Mornin', y'all," I said calmly, as if Noah Blore showed up in my kitchen every day of the week.

"It's hardly morning, Pidge," Aunt Retta said, with a trace of a smile. "It's after twelve o'clock. Catchin' up on your beauty sleep, were you?"

Little Jack nearly fell out of his chair. "Hope she keeps runnin', 'cause I don't think she's caught it yet!"

I glared at him, and Noah laughed out loud. Shoot. I didn't know which person in this room to maim first.

Papa took a long swig of coffee and stood up. "Well, I got me some farming to do, now that the rain's finally stopped. Nice seein' you again, Noah."

Noah nodded uncomfortably. "Same to you, Mr. Martin." Then he shifted his gaze to me. "Thought you might want to go see Big Al and her babies, over at Sinkhole Lake," he said. "Water's come up about three feet with the rain and all."

Little Jack jumped to his feet, all excited. "Can I go, too?" he said, but Aunt Retta grabbed his arm, forcing him back down.

"I don't believe you were invited," she said pointedly.

Noah's eyes hurriedly scanned the room, as if searching for a quick way out. Leastways, they sure weren't looking at me. Well, one thing was for certain. *I* wanted to get out of here as much as he did.

"All right. Let's go then," I said quickly. I took four giant steps toward the back door, not even daring to peek back and see if Noah was following me. He was.

"Wait up, Pidge," he called, as I marched across the porch and around the house. "This ain't a contest, you know."

I slowed, allowing him to catch up with me. Then we walked for a while, not saying anything, simply letting our feet carry us through the woods and over the familiar path to the lake.

"Hey," he spoke up finally.

"Hey, yourself," I countered, wondering if this might not be a contest after all.

"I liked your mama's jewelry," he said, and I had to laugh a little.

"Did Little Jack bore you with all that stuff?" I said, embarrassed.

"It wasn't boring," he said. "He was real proud of it. Showed me every last thing in that box."

I rolled my eyes, and Noah stopped walking.

"He also told me that your mama . . . well . . ."

"What? Killed herself?" I said angrily.

"*What?* No! Why would Little Jack—"

"Well, she didn't! Mama was depressed, and that's what killed her. It's nothing to be ashamed of. So maybe you can go back and tell Dora all about it."

Noah took a startled step backward, as if I might be the crazy one. "You could always tell her yourself," he said quietly, his eyes not leaving mine.

"Maybe I will," I said, and we kept on walking.

When we got to the lake, I saw that the water was dark and deep, the way it always was just before the leaves in the trees started to change color. And as I stared down into the murky water, a sadness overtook me, a sense that everything was changing and I could do nothing to stop it. The weather, the seasons, Little Jack, my father and Miss Jenny, even my feelings about Dora. And about her father. I just couldn't keep up.

What was it Papa had said to me the other night?

*Things change all the time. And that's the way it should be.* Well. Maybe I was changing, too.

Noah stepped up to the water's edge, next to me, and I felt his arm brush against mine. I stood very still, holding my breath, willing him to take my fingers into the warm cocoon of his hand.

And he did. We stood that way, hand in hand, for what seemed like hours. But I think that was only because my heart was beating so fast.

"I think they're gone," he said at last.

"Who?" I asked, forgetting what we had trekked all this way to see.

Noah laughed. "Big Al and her babies. Isn't that what we came here for?"

I smiled at him then, feeling the warmth of his hand coursing through my own. "Was it?" I asked, and he laughed again.

"Partly," he said, giving my fingers a slight squeeze.

We gazed out over the water again, both of us wondering what to do next.

"Maybe she just decided it was time to take her babies and move on," I said.

"Probably," he agreed.

At that precise moment, a shaft of light broke through the trees and floated across the surface of the water like a ribbon. It looked to me like an endless ribbon of light, wrapping around the lake and around me and Noah, too. I followed the ribbon with my eyes, as it skimmed across the water and up over the edges of the trees, up and up into the sky, where it began. Where everything began. And I felt its light entering me, filling me until I was fit to burst, ready to let everything go. Just like the rain clouds.

I thought—for just one moment—that I might actually know how Miss Millie's magic worked. How she knew—without even knowing she knew—when it was time for the rain to just let go and be set free. Like that last drop on a penny. But then the feeling was gone, and the ribbon passed on, over the ground and into the darkness of the woods. The magic had disappeared, if it had ever really existed at all.

Noah shivered beside me, and I knew that he had felt it, too. That something had entered the two of us. That maybe it had been there all the time.

But we couldn't talk about it. Not now. It was still too new, and too wonderful.

So we simply stood and watched the water as it rose and fell with the breeze, my fingers swallowed up in his own until our two hands fit together. Like a seamless piece of fine fabric, wrapping around us both.

And for now, that was magic enough for me.

# Author's Note

To the best of my knowledge, there is no town called "Frostfree" in Florida, nor has there ever been. But dozens of small farming towns just like it have existed for decades throughout the central part of the state. Long before theme parks and tourism, citrus farming was the major business in central Florida, and a great deal of the local farmers' success depended upon the weather.

Rain was particularly scarce during the spring of 1939. And in an act of desperation, a Florida citrus baron named Philip Phillips brought a "Rainmaker" to what was then only the small farming town of Orlando. Miss Lillie Stoate of Oxford, Mississippi, was summoned by Dr. Phillips during that spring of

1939, and she caused quite a sensation. The woman was sixty-seven years old and nearly deaf, but by the time she reached Orlando on April 6, the "Rainmaker" was front-page news. And in a town already hard hit by the economic Depression and a war escalating in Europe, Miss Lillie was welcome news indeed.

Her method was simply to plant herself in one spot—in this instance, beside the shores of Sand Lake—and to busy herself by reading the paper, eating strawberries, or quietly sitting. The Rainmaker did not use incantations, rain dances, or secret potions. She merely "projected herself into the firmament" in order to bring the rain that citrus growers so desperately needed.

Miss Lillie's method seemed to work, for within twenty-four hours of her arrival, heavy rains and showers poured down upon the Orlando area. Headlines from the day after Miss Lillie's historic vigil read: "Rainmaker's Charms Work in Orlando" and "Rainmaker Brings 'Pennies from Heaven'"—referring to a song especially popular during the Depression years.

But that was not the end of it, by any means. After the Rainmaker's visit, Dr. Phillips was approached by a local naysayer who criticized him, declaring Miss Lillie's methods to be nothing but "witchcraft against science." The Florida citrus grower disagreed. And he offered ten thousand dollars in cash to anyone who could prove conclusively that Miss Stoate did not bring the rain.

A fellow named Dr. Leo S. Wheeler stepped forward to challenge Phillips, asking him to give the money to a local children's charity. But Dr. Phillips refused. It had rained within twenty-four hours of Miss Lillie's arrival, he said, and that was proof enough for him.

Lillie Stoate returned to her hometown of Oxford, Mississippi, where she died on December 3, 1946. The orange groves once owned by Dr. Phillips were eventually sold and commercially developed. They have now been replaced by homes, hotels, shopping malls, and Universal Studios, Orlando.